Incandescence

Also by Tracey-Anne Forbes and published by Ginninderra Press
Crushed Sugar
Saving Ginia
Dangerous Places

Tracey-Anne Forbes

Incandescence

The characters and events in this story are fictitious and any resemblance to real people or events is purely coincidental.

Incandescence
ISBN 978 1 76109 601 3
Copyright © text Tracey-Anne Forbes 2023
Cover image: Chris from Pixabay

First published 2023 by
GINNINDERRA PRESS
PO Box 3461 Port Adelaide 5015
www.ginninderrapress.com.au

Contents

1

La Charité

At two forty-three a.m., the moon spikes ice-light through the lace curtain above Odette's pillow. Since midnight she has been fitfully aware of the thin glow drifting, like despair, across the outer world toward the inner: shifting in shade as the hands of her watch have shifted in shape with each twitched start of her freezing calf muscles.

And so, at two forty-three, with the moon patterned upon her, Odette gives up. She drags her body upright. Her muscles ache from their tension at the cold; her breath she sees in the moonlight is a long stream of vapour.

Beside her, Jason stirs and whimpers. He snuggles into her hip, searching for the warmth and comfort of her breast. Odette shivers, braces herself: raises her heavy jumper, the sweater underneath, the singlet beneath that. She lifts him onto her lap and he nuzzles, finding the breast instinctively. While he feeds, she rubs his legs through their sleeping suit and tucks his cold hands between her jumper and sweater. She can't tell whether his nappy is dry or wet, her fingers are so numb; but if she changed it, she would wake him properly, so she lets it be. She fusses with the hood of his suit.

She huddles with him, and leans her head against the lace. It doesn't move under her hair. Puzzled, she turns to it and finds that the curtain has frozen onto the glass; she touches it and tugs it away and sees that the pattern of the lace has been etched on the window in ice.

When Jason is asleep, she puts him down beside her again and piles as much of the slack of their sleeping bag around him as she can. Then she turns automatically to drink from the cup of water on the corner bench beside her – and gags on chips of ice.

And her forbearance cracks like a mirror.

It's the end. *It's intolerable.* Odette sobs, a sob almost of grief, of frustration and despair and powerlessness; but her eyes are so dry and sharp, warm tears won't even form in them. I should not be here, she thinks. *I should not be here*, frozen, risking my baby's *life* perhaps, not able to sleep, not able to eat properly because Megan has been hell-bent on tearing down here on a stupid goose chase that's bound to fail, *making* me, making me have to face *him* again – and now, not even able to *drink water* to replenish my milk, not even to have that basic necessity for my baby…

She shudders and huddles, struggling with the cold ache in her throat. Breathes deeply: smoothes the wrinkled panic. Calms. And thinks, all right. All right. I have no control over this. At least, not much. Not yet. But let's get this into perspective. Water, first. All right, it's cold. It's becoming frozen. And if I tip that frozen water into me, I'll be even more chilled. But I'm thirsty, whether from habit or need; and freezing beyond belief. All right.

At the back of the bench, the top part of a laminate frame around a gas-powered refrigerator, there are various bottles of Megan's. Whisky, gin and cognac. Duty free: some from Australia, some from the ferry port at Dover. The EEC: no one checks. Anyway, Odette had not wanted anything, not while she's breastfeeding, so it was probably all legal. All right, Odette thinks. They say St Bernard dogs searching for the lost in the snow carry brandy.

She reaches determinedly for the cognac: uncorks it, and tips the bottle at her lips. And the hot, almost sweet drink runs down her throat like liquid steam. She sighs, and closes her eyes with her hair against the frozen window. Breathes in the fumes. Feels the fire in the liquor stimulate her heart, her lungs, almost her fingertips.

There. She pours a little more cognac into the water cup, waits, then swallows two mouthfuls. The mixture is almost drinkable.

The next thing is the cold. There must be some way of warming up. Her sleeping bag, warm and cosy on a winter camp in Australia, when she and Matt had taken a borrowed four-wheel drive and tent to Fraser Island, and warm enough for the night she and Megan and Jason spent in Dover, is like a thin sheet against this temperature. They have a small gas heater in the van, but it is stored under one of the seats which make up the head and tail of her bed, so is difficult to get at without waking Jason, and Megan has turned the gas off for the night as well. Besides, they have hardly any gas left. Megan would not approve.

Extra covering, then. Her coat! Easing herself over the sleeping Jason, she kneels and leans awkwardly to rummage in a narrow closet set in the space between the van cockpit and this, its cabin, or living area. And, blindly, seems to take ridiculously long to seize upon what should be easily distinguished from the other garments, because of its fake-fur lining and heaviness.

She drags it out and bundles it over them. Immediately, the weight of cold seems to lift. She thinks, why didn't I do this hours ago? And sighs again. For the same reason she often tossed fretfully in the dark in the flat in Rockhampton, brushing away mosquitoes instead of switching on the light and dealing with them properly; or lay sleeplessly, tense, listening to sounds which seemed to be in the house...

No. Better not to get onto that. She'd never get to sleep if she started thinking about that. About Dickson. Leave that to Megan.

The first effects of the cognac recede, leaving Odette suddenly drowsy. Her eyes, instead of being coldly dry, feel heavy and hot. Better. Much better. She finishes the rest of her cup and wriggles down until her head is on the pillow; she curls her body around her baby, and sleeps.

*

Jason wakes her at daybreak – eight a.m. Despite the sounds he makes – gurgles of delight, mainly, at finding himself in bed with her, and then snuffling noises as he finds her breast – there is no movement from the bunk above the cockpit: only a still lump and silence. Megan's as bad as Matt, Odette thinks: he never woke to Jason's demands either. Just slept blissfully on. Matt.

She huddles, miserable suddenly. It's partly the let-down effect of her milk, she recognises. That always gives her a wave of fatigue, of something like despair. Partly.

There are grey velvet curtains half pulled across the lace ones behind her head; she pushes them open and stares blearily out the window. The dawn light is pale and weak, but bright enough for her to see, through the frosting of ice on the glass, the bleakness of their campsite.

A deserted tyre yard. At least, it was deserted yesterday. After driving south from Calais for most of the day, on slippery, ice-edged roads, they had, tired and hungry, searched for a camping ground near Nevers; but they had run up blind alleys, then followed camping signs which led nowhere or to *fermé* – closed for the winter – notices. And then they had found themselves on a narrow country lane heading out of town – in the wrong direction. And as the sun was setting, they had come across this. So this is where Megan had decided to pull up. And Jason had needed feeding, needed changing: Odette had agreed.

There was a tap, but that was about all the place had going for it. Odette had walked around the yard, walked up the road a little to stretch legs cramped from travelling all day; and discovered that the roadside was littered with broken beer bottles, cigarette packets and scraps of food packaging. Then the surrounding fields were winter-barren, and a wind brittle with cold had blown straight across them to rock the van. The patch of bitumen on which they'd parked was stained with streaks of oil and the piled, strapped tyres reeked of used-car lots, of sad, bleak urbanity and sterile industry.

Megan had been brisk and businesslike, however, and of course that was the only way to be: she had filled their water tank from the tap and under cover of darkness emptied their port-a-pottee after digging a pit in a neighbouring field. Odette had taken her cue and made soup, which warmed the van as well as their bodies; then she'd heated water in saucepans on the van's stove to wash the dishes, to bath Jason, and finally so that she and Megan could take it in turn to squat shivering over a plastic tub to wash their armpits and bottoms.

Then they had retired, each to her bunk, to stare into the darkness and eventually to sleep. And the cold had settled and seeped in and frozen the van.

And now it is morning. And still bitterly cold. Odette finishes feeding Jason and changes his nappy and his clothes as quickly as she can, with her legs still encased in her sleeping bag. Then she sits him up and props pillows behind him, and rucks the sleeping bag around his legs. He watches her, chewing on a plastic toy, his eyes bright and very blue and so like Matt's she feels a spasm of courage.

She undresses hastily: tearing off the last layer with a gasp. She has one set of clean clothes left: a heavy velvet skirt and a singlet and woollen tights and one of Matt's jumpers; the coat encases it all, and her old Doc Marten's go with everything, or nothing.

Then as she ties her laces there is a rap on the camper van door.

'*Bonjour, mam'selle.*' The voice is deep, growly, issuing from his mouth in a dragon-puff of steam; his face has grey, spiky whiskers and a fleshy nose and eyes as faded as his stained jeans.

She watches him take in the room behind her, then sees his suspicion lift as his eyes alight on Jason.

He glances back at her, and this time his expression is puzzled. '*Mais qu'est-ce que vous faites ici?*'

'I'm sorry.' She looks nervously back into the van, and is rewarded with a movement from the lump on the bunk above the cockpit. 'I don't speak French – Megan does – we're Australian…'

'*Ici, c'est privée, vous savez. Il y a des campings…*'

'*Tous les campings sont fermés!*' Megan's voice is abrupt and rapid.

Odette and the Frenchman turn to it in unison and even Jason swings his head up. '*Je m'excuse si ça vous dérange, mais nous n'avions pas de choix. On part bientôt, en tout cas. Il faut dormir, comme même, hien?*'

The old man lifts his frown from her tousled head back to Odette. After a pause he says, addressing Odette, '*Où allez-vous?*'

'*Nous allons au sud! En Espagne.*'

Again the old man frowns at Megan; he looks at Jason, and back at

Odette. He hesitates, then abruptly swings away from the doorway and snaps, *'Bon! Tant mieux!'*

Odette watches him stamp off down the road; once, he throws a glance back at her, and, catching her eye, shakes his head.

'What was all that about?'

Megan is easing herself down from the bunk, still in her sleeping bag. 'Brrr! Can you get the stove on? This van is like a freezer. He just wanted to know what we're doing here – reckoned we should be in a camping ground. I told him there weren't any open and we had to sleep somewhere and we're leaving soon anyway. What's his problem? It's Christmas Eve, for Christ's sake! Nobody's working here today. And it's hardly a bloody paradise we're polluting with our presence. What's up?'

'I can't get the tap to pump…'

'What?' Megan hobbles to the sink in the sleeping bag.

They stand side by side, Odette irresolute, her hands hanging, Megan working the pump with humped shoulders, her straight wedged blonde hair swinging rhythmically. Nothing happens.

Megan's hands still, and she uncurls her body slowly. 'You know what the problem is, don't you? The water in the tank's frozen.'

They stare at each other.

Then Megan says slowly, 'I'd better see if I can get the motor to start, hey?'

Odette goes to follow her out the van door, but Jason whimpers. By the time she has scooped him up and eased both of them over the ice-covered van step, Megan is already in the cockpit, her thumb on the diesel button.

Odette huddles uselessly with her baby inside her coat. There is ice on everything: ice puddles on the bitumen, a rind of ice on the dark green hedge between the tyre yard and the neighbouring field, white patches like calamine lotion on the face of the bare earth of the field. When Odette bends to a tuft of grass, she sees the ice has turned it to glass. She can't feel anything with her fingers; her body shakes inside so that she quivers; her feet, numb with cold all night, are clumsy and foreign still. Oh, tea, she thinks; what I would give for hot tea. The engine strains under Megan's thumb.

She can't see Megan through the windscreen because ice has frosted over it. How are they to dissolve it, without warm water? Should they try the yard tap for water? But what if the pipes there are frozen too, and they damage them? It's too risky. How then? Can they scrape it off somehow?

She fetches a blunt knife from the cabin and, still with Jason on her hip, starts chipping at the ice on the driver's side. But it's useless. Even without Jason beginning to whinge, even without her clumsy, frozen fingers, it would take her a week to clear the glass.

The engine labours, pauses, labours. Odette opens the driver door and she and Megan stare wordlessly at each other.

Then Megan half-smiles. 'Don't look so worried. It'll start. My father had a diesel once. They can take a while to warm up, but you can't flood the engine. Once she starts, we'll get the heaters on and defrost it in no time. How about making something to eat so once she gets going we can hit the road and melt the water? Stop for a cup of coffee then.'

The knife in Odette's hand looks childish. She turns quickly and goes back to the cabin. She can't heat anything on the stove because the gas must be turned off for the engine to start, so she butters a baguette and spreads jam thickly on it and as she wraps the sandwiches in a tea towel, the motor splutters and roars. Odette stands with Jason strapped in a sling to her chest and the food parcel in her hands, and closes her eyes.

2

Checy

Only when the pain from the denumbing of her hands and feet has receded does Odette brace herself to confront Megan. Warm hands, a quiet, warm baby and the bulky, sweet breakfast combine to strengthen her courage. 'I think we should stop,' she says abruptly.

'Stop? Now?' Megan keeps her eyes on the snow-edged road ahead, but frowns.

'No. For Christmas.'

'But –'

'He won't be going anywhere for a while. He can't, can he? It's Christmas tomorrow, Jason's first Christmas – and I haven't got anything for him, and we haven't got anything for ourselves.' Odette's voice is firm, but she looks straight ahead. 'We should have been back by now –'

'You think I want to be here any more than you do? But we agreed to this. The paper's paid our fares – we can't just go back without finding him!'

'I know.' Odette's voice is resigned and quiet. 'But no one said we couldn't stop for Christmas. Everyone stops for Christmas. Besides, we need gas and food – we've got to live. And no one said we shouldn't enjoy at least parts of this – I may never come back – and let's face it, there's nothing for either of us to race back for. Is there?'

Megan raises an eyebrow at the road. Shrewd move, she thinks, but doesn't say.

'Look.' Odette's voice is beginning to strain. 'Stopping for one day's not going to make any difference. One day: to shop, to do our washing in a laundromat, to eat, to sleep –'

Megan throws a quick glance at Odette then. The skin around her eyes is pinched and dry, and the bones in her face protrude in shadowed ridges. The baby's waking in the night hasn't escaped Megan: but it hasn't kept her awake for more than a couple of minutes either. Unlike Odette. How she has enough milk in that slight frame to feed such a robust child...

And of course Jason's probably not the only one keeping her awake, either. Odette hasn't said much, but the thought of seeing Dickson again, of the interview with him hanging over her, with so much resting on it... No wonder she wants to put it off.

Megan sighs. It would have been so much easier to have just come by herself; but then would she have been able to accomplish anything that way? No; Odette and the baby were necessary. She'd been over that a hundred times with Pete before they'd left. Odette could make all the difference. If she didn't crack. If only bloody Dickson had stayed that extra day in London, if he hadn't cut his week there short and disappeared. So they'd spent three days trying to track him down. If only Pete had believed in this story more, had been willing to pay their extra airfares to Spain and for hotels there – but he hadn't. He'd tried to get her to drop the story when the police department closed ranks; and he didn't have any more faith in the idea of Odette getting anywhere – thought that Dickson would be too sharp for them.

Pete could be talked into paying for their airfares from Australia and a couple of days accommodation in a B&B in London only because he had a good deal going with one of the airlines – and then she'd managed to talk him into paying for one week's hire of a camping van once they'd traced Dickson's whereabouts – but he'd drawn the line at anything more. He'd suspected that Megan wanted to come to Europe for more than this story too...there at least he'd been perceptive.

'Okay.'

Odette jolts in surprise, and relief.

'Okay.' Megan slows the van and pulls off the road, but she leaves the engine idling. She turns to face Odette, her shoulders hunched against the van door, her straight fair hair smooth and neat around her face, like a doll's. 'We can do that.' She pauses for a moment, frowning slightly. 'In fact, it's probably not a bad idea if we lie low for a couple of days. Look – I didn't tell you, but when I rang that contact of Pete's in Alicante yesterday, he told me he wasn't sure where Dickson was.'

'What?' Odette's voice is incredulous; her arms tighten around Jason, who lifts his face to hers in response.

'Don't panic. He is in Alicante. It's just he's not staying with the relatives they thought he'd go to. But he will go to them eventually – his stuff's still there. Or Pete's contact will track him down. But whichever way, there's probably no great need to go hurtling down there. Not if you don't want to. Now.' Megan, her heart quickening, looks at Odette fully. 'What we could do is – go back to Orléans.'

'Orléans? But why?'

'Well, see –' Megan drops her gaze and turns her face away from Odette's frown, to profile – 'once we'd seen Dickson in London, I was going to come over here, to France, anyway. Told Pete I'd get a back-up story, just in case. On French domestic castles: something we could use, regardless. In the travel pages. I know someone over here: Luc Dubois. I'd arranged to see him Boxing Day. I was going to change that tonight, phone him, see if I could meet him closer to New Year. But we could go back. He's in Orléans, about fifty k back north, I'd say. Find a camping ground near there, spend Christmas there, then see him. Kill two birds with one stone.'

Odette's face clears a little: she notes the faint pink in Megan's cheeks as Megan glances back at her. Ah, she thinks: I knew there was something she hadn't told me.

'Well?'

Odette colours, herself, at Megan's abrupt tone. 'Oh, yes, yes, that sounds just right…'

'Right.' Megan turns back to face the steering wheel and revs the engine, brisk again. 'Well, they're bound to have some sort of shopping centre somewhere near Orléans. Probably outside it, from what we've seen so far. They seem to have as much centralised shopping as we do

– bloody supermarkets in razed-earth policy landscapes with as much character as a plastic batman – I wouldn't have believed the French could've let it happen if I hadn't met some of them recently. But anyway, we'll find one of those and get the washing on, then do some shopping. Then we'll look around for a real camping ground. If we can find one, we'll stop till Boxing Day. All right?'

'Yeah, yeah – great. Thanks.' Odette slides her eyes sideways as Megan swings the van into a U-turn, and watches her relax back into her bucket seat and the muscles of her face untighten for the first time in days.

*

They watch the road in silence, lulled by the warmth of the van's heater and the throb of its engine. The bitumen unskeins before them, lined completely as an avenue is with precisely symmetrically placed trees, all with a white stripe of snow down the southern side, as if the keepers of the trees (for surely there must be such keepers to plant and prune such trees) have also painted on the snow. The sky is watery blue, a pale, pale pastel; the landscape on either side of the road is neutral, all black and white, except for clumps of fir trees laden like fake Christmas trees with unreal snow. Occasionally there is a castle, or the ruins of one, standing bleakly and coldly against the sky. Jason sleeps, strapped in his sling to Odette, her seat belt threaded firmly between her body and his. It's not really safe, but it's the best she can do; they hadn't been able to find such a thing as a baby seat in their hurried travels around London. The van won't do over eighty most of the time anyway, so she takes comfort in that.

She watches the road, and gradually her eyes close.

*

Megan drives steadily. Once, she glances briefly at the map which has fallen from Odette's fingers onto the handbrake, and grimaces. How strange, she thinks, that Odette should decide she wants to stop now.

Or is it so strange? After all, it was she, Megan, who had made the decision to hurtle from London so quickly that it was almost impossible not to stop at this point, she who had decided on this roundabout route to Spain. The frozen water tank was not her doing, nor the proximity of Christmas, nor the slippery roads and the cold and the need, just for a few days, for shelter in a camping ground: those were the hand of fate, the cruel hand, perhaps…

Because he might be hostile to her. Or might regard her with amusement, see the whole article as a ploy on her part to see him again. No, no, he would know it was not her doing, that it was his mother's doing, in fact. Indirectly. And for all he knew, she was happily ensconced in a relationship in Australia. But then he might resent the time he was giving up for her, particularly in his holidays…

Stop, Megan tells herself. Stop! You'll talk yourself out of it in a minute. And then she sees that she does actually have to stop, because there on her right is a huge billboard in green, red and white saying *Supermarche Prisunic, 2 km à Checy – Chateauneuf 10 km*; and indeed within two kilometres, just within the boundary of the little village of Checy, the supermarket looms.

*

Megan pulls into the car park, then hesitates with the engine still running. 'Look, there's no point in both of us going in. How about I scout around and see if I can find out about a camping ground? And look for a laundromat? Meet you back here in, say, an hour? Okay? Here's a thousand francs. And you'd better take the empty gas bottle: the van hire company said you simply exchange the old for a new, and that way you only have to pay for the gas itself.' Her voice is cheerful.

Odette, dazed a little from being woken abruptly, is searching in a bag on the floor for a clean nappy: she sits upright and nods briefly in reply; but there is panic in her throat. How will she cope, she thinks, not speaking French? But it's a supermarket after all – everything prepackaged and labelled with prices… She takes the offered money and, holding Jason still strapped to her chest, steps out of the van into the frosty morning before she can change her mind.

Jason wakes as soon as the cold air hits them; his breath curls under her chin and around her ears as he cries. Odette bundles her coat around him and hurries across the expanse of car park, lugging the gas bottle; and then they are through automatic doors and inside.

And it is all foreign, and yet so familiar. There's the huge food shop, with its checkouts and trolleys; there are specialty shops with their peculiarly mixed smells – bakers and flower shops and boutiques selling scarves and hats and shoes – and there, as if conjured up by wishing, is a sign for toilets and a baby changing room.

The relief of changing Jason without him wailing from the cold, and of sitting in a quiet, warm room to feed him, and of washing both of their faces and hands in warm, running water makes Odette feel like someone released from a prison. And then, entering the food shop, her heart gives a leap of excitement.

The trolleys are tricky: she has to drop a franc into a slot to free one, she finds, after watching other shoppers. She will get the franc back when she returns the trolley to its rank. Fortunately, she has some change in her purse, from an exchange she made to buy coffee on the ferry from Dover.

She lowers the empty gas bottle into the trolley, then props Jason up in the child seat, bundling the nappy bag around him to stop him falling sideways. His back is strengthening, but he is still prone to topple. She wheels the trolley to the end aisle, and, with a breath of resolution, begins.

She buys little dried biscuits shaped like tiny slices of toast, a cognac-flavoured pâté, a thick wedge of Camembert cheese; a chicken, head and claws intact, potatoes, carrots and broccoli, nectarines and oranges and strawberries; almond pastries and long loaves of bread and fresh butter; sherry and champagne and red and white wine; a whole frozen Alaskan salmon from the fish-fragrant display along the entire back wall of the shop; tins of tomatoes and artichoke hearts and asparagus and baby food… In the final aisles, she finds camping gas, hot water bottles, a thermos – and toys. With a rush of final extravagance, she puts in a toy telephone which rings and when answered responds in French, a set of Duplo building blocks, and a fluffy brown toy squirrel with huge soft eyes. She may not have enough, of course…

But the bill comes to nine hundred and fifty francs.

*

Then out in the cold car park, Odette's flush of excitement at her purchases freezes into panic. There is no sign of the van. She stands quite still in the spot where Megan dropped her, more than an hour ago, the loaded plastic bags in their trolley rustling in a sharp gust of wind. What, she thinks, if Megan is lost? Or has had an accident? Is lying injured somewhere… She has Odette's passport. Her clothes, everything…

And then the van appears.

Megan throws open the back door, leaving the engine idling. 'You won't believe it!' she cries, before Odette can speak. 'There's a four-star campsite on the river near here, that's about fifteen dollars a night, with hot showers, *and* a laundry! Open! Unbelievable! How'd you go? Jesus! What have you *got* in all this?'

'Enough to give us a decent Christmas, and get us through to Alicante, hopefully. Here's the change.' Odette hands Megan the fifty francs.

Megan frowns at it, then at Odette's pink face with Jason's solemn one nestled under it; she closes her mouth, and bends to take the bags Odette offers.

*

The river is grey in its smooth, unruffled patches, and like milk-blue, rucked satin under the agitation of wind gusts: it could be a mudflat, Odette thinks, only the water is deep, you can see from the current, not shallow at all.

The wind washes against her face like iced water. There are high, frozen wastes of cloud, ice-white, stretched and snapped like white pastry rolled too thinly. Perhaps, perhaps, tomorrow it will snow? The Frenchman who booked them in told Megan a white Christmas was forecast. That would make up in part for the cold, the discomfort of the van, the stress of trying to keep their bodies and clothes clean. Odette shoves her gloved hands deeper into the pockets of her coat and turns with a lighter heart from her river walk toward the anticipation of a fragrant van warmed by a beef casserole she has left bubbling in red wine and mushrooms, under Megan's care. If it wasn't for the shadow of Dickson falling across the horizon of the week, she could almost be happy.

*

At midnight, the church bells in the village of Checy begin to peal. Throughout the night, intermittently they ring out again, but they disturb only Odette, who stirs blearily and briefly to check that Jason, tucked between her body and a hot water bottle, is still actually sleeping. It is only at daybreak, stretching and propping herself up to breastfeed, that Odette pushes back the van curtain to reveal the frosting of white on cars, caravans, hedges and a soccer field, and on their own van.

And immediately, resolutely, as if she has promised herself this beforehand, which perhaps subconsciously she has, she thinks, I won't let Dickson worry me today. Today, I won't think of him once. I won't think of Matt, where Matt is this Christmas Day when he should have been with us, either. This is a magic Christmas, an unlikely gift stolen from the purse of the blue witch of the north, and I will treat it as such and enjoy it and remember it so that one thing good at least will emerge from all this…

'Away in a manger,' she begins to sing, softly cradling her blue-eyed child to her other breast, 'no crib for a bed', and as she sings she maps out the day so it will be as perfect a strange Christmas as its strangeness will allow. She will, she thinks, cook eggs and brew real coffee; then prepare and baste the chicken and put it into their van oven to roast in sherry; and then they will dress up and walk along the ice-grey Loire in the crisp air and across snow-crunching fields to the village where they can both ring home, and then perhaps find a Christmas service in a church or chapel; and then she will peel potatoes and carrots and roast those too and Jason will have his tin of turkey and vegetable puree and sleep in the afternoon and she and Megan will drink real French champagne and for dessert they will have almond pastries and custard tarts and more real coffee, and perhaps cognac.

3

Christmas

'That was wonderful. Where'd you learn to make a meal like that?' Megan, lying along the cushions on her side of the van's collapsible table, sips her tumbler of cognac and flops her head back against the cabin wall.

Odette looks up from arranging herself to feed Jason. 'Oh, I've always loved cooking. Did Home Ec. at school – tried out lots of recipes on my family. Mum didn't mind – she's a typical Biloela cook. Good at steak and mashed potato and lamingtons.'

Megan nods with a grimace and sips again. The table is scattered with the remains of their Christmas dinner – gravy-streaked plates and bottles and glasses and half-eaten pastries and a bowl of nectarines and strawberries – and Megan lazily thinks that she should clean it all up. But for the first time in years, it seems, she feels comforted; comforted as she was as a child by the warmth of hot Sunday dinners in winter with both her parents, before her mother died, the peaceful and lazy unfurling of languid afternoons spent making jigsaw puzzles while her parents drank tea and chattered, one on each side of her.

Megan watches Odette settle Jason to her breast and feels almost tenderly toward her. She's like a bird, Megan thinks; or was, at one time that morning while contemplating the river, like a bird about to take flight over it…or now, like a swan, with her long neck arched over the child. Her spine has a slight curve to it, like a beautifully formed comma. She has black, high-arched, winged eyebrows and very pale skin. Her hair is long and black and straight. No wonder, Megan thinks suddenly, that bastard wanted her: she has a dreamy, elusive quality, a fragility difficult to interpret, the pliable, gentle passivity of a victim.

And, Megan thinks, I am not at all like that. I'm narrow and thin but strong and assertive: I know my rights in the world and no one would dare challenge them. She wriggles a little then, drawing herself up, flipping a strand of hair, of which she is suddenly conscious, from her face; and she thinks, they're masculine qualities: all right, but we live in a masculine world, where only competition and ambition and aggression really count, and if Odette had been a bit more aggressive, Megan switches, suddenly, half-angry, we wouldn't be here in the first place…

Here.

In France. In this country I have an obsession with, because it is the country of my mother's birth, even though she was by all other accounts English, brought up from the age of seven in England and married to an Englishman, however working class, and adopting English habits. Thoroughly English, even though they emigrated with two-year-old me to Australia in the late sixties. In this country where I have half-wanted to belong, half-found alien and rigid and self-obsessed – where I half-fell in love with the only other male besides David who has ever haunted my dreams.

She sighs, aware of a skipped heartbeat; and the anger, which is only token anyway, dissipates. She glances out of the van window at the snow, grey-brown through the tinted glass, gently drifting behind it. She thinks, now what the hell am I getting nervous about? Or, if I must be truthful, excited about? All right, Luc's single. His two-year relationship broke up. He's at a loose end. He remembers me. Wrote to me. Would love to see me again, introduce me to castle-owners. And he sent me three years ago, out of the blue, a magazine with that poem he sang to me published in it, with just 'I'm sorry'… So what? He had an attack of conscience, that's all; and now he's being polite. Doing the polite French patriotic thing. But what luck, what luck the Ravels are away; although I might have been able to meet up with him in any case – I did want to, just out of curiosity really, find out why he…

'So what's his name again, this man you're going to see tomorrow? How do you know him?'

It's as if Odette has read her mind: Megan glances up sharply, but Odette's face is innocent of guile.

'Luc Dubois.' She says the name abruptly. 'I knew him, oh, ten years ago, more or less. When I was a bit younger than you. I was an au pair girl for friends of his mother. The only way I could convince Pete to pay for our fares over here was if I arranged a back-up feature article on something to do with France or Spain – we agreed castles always get the nod. So, I wrote to the Ravels – the family I au paired for – but they were going to Canada. Luc's a bit of a French history buff, so they asked him if he'd help me instead. He lives in Paris, but his father and stepmother live in Orléans. He's staying with them for Christmas.'

She wriggles again, pulling her body upright, unconsciously straightening her shoulders. 'I think I should see him like I planned, tomorrow, don't you think? The roads are going to be very slippery, and if it's like this here, what's it going to be like crossing the Massif Central? He mightn't have the time later – he's probably made plans for the rest of the holiday.' She meets Odette's eye sharply, aware of her own over-justification.

But Odette only smiles back, warmly, lifting Jason onto her shoulder to burp him. 'Of course you should see him,' she says. 'We've already agreed about that. You should ring him, though, and let him know you're here, if you have his number.'

Megan shrugs and picks up her cognac; then she semi-nods. 'Of course. I was going to do that.'

*

When Jason is asleep and the van is cleared and Megan has stomped out into the snow, Odette takes out a notebook, a sort of diary which she has been keeping on and off since she was at school: this book not a formal, hardbacked diary like the ones she received as presents when she was a child, and which her older sister discovered and read aloud one day as entertainment for her friends, who rolled with mirth and sibling rivalry revenge – no, this is a nondescript book with lined pages and a soft cardboard cover. It is a book she is using as a sort of escape – a way of escaping the present, ironically – a book she is using in the same way she uses cooking to escape reality: when she cooks or writes, she can imagine her life anywhere as being as she would wish.

She reads her last entry.

London. It's tall, and narrow, and grey and black and white; it smells of diesel and carbon dioxide and snow, I think – a strange, cold scent that almost hurts the inside of your nose, but that's tinged with some sort of vague, anticipatory sort of…excitement. We are staying at a bed-and-breakfast place near Victoria Station. Megan knows this area; she's been here before. She's so efficient she overwhelms me. I just tag along behind her like a puppy.

The B&B has four storeys and a basement, which is where we have breakfast. The top three floors each had three bedrooms and one communal bathroom. Our bedroom is on the third floor: it has a single bed for Megan and a double that I sleep in with Jason. The bathroom… Oh, what a bathroom. It is Victorian, clean and warm! The bath has a marvelous, flattened broad tap, like a broad, broken nose, which gushes hot, hot water. The fittings are all in chrome. There are cream tiles to the roof. The hem of the window curtains is hand-stitched. There is no mirror, but the toilet has a wooden seat and the bath and sink are real porcelain and there are brass curtain rods and a brass runner around the roof above the bath for the shower curtain to be pulled across. Best of all, a three-bar heater above the door.

I have spent three days here with Jason, while Megan is out, tracking down Dickson, and now trying to rent a van: bracing her face for the north wind, catching tubes and buses and cursing us all, no doubt.

And so tomorrow we leave for Alicante. And there, face the nightmare again.

Odette, remembering her morning resolution, and helped by the euphoria of heavy food and wine to keep to it, carefully skips over the last line, and grimaces. You didn't even know what cold *meant*! she thinks. And oh, for that bathroom now. But never mind: the van is warm and there are hot showers in the campsite: small mercies. And it's been a lovely Christmas Day, really, despite everything.

Christmas Day. She leans back against the lace curtain, lowers the notebook to her lap, and closes her eyes; and thinks about how she and Jason would have spent the day if they'd been in Australia. In Biloela. With her mother and sisters, everyone fussing over Jason and her nieces and nephews; and a hot, late roast lunch of turkey and greasy pork and flamed plum pudding, with a giant, industrial fan her mother picked up at an auction whirling noisy, hot air at their clothes and hair, and blowing off their pulled-cracker paper hats.

Swims in the tepid pool: dazzling white light dancing on the water and the smell of chlorine and rubber inflatable mats and frangipani; hot towels, baking brick paths, glaring concrete around the pool bubbling when water splashes it. Scarcely veiled comments about Matt from her mother, who'd disapproved of Odette leaving Biloela to start with, disapproved of her going to uni in Rockhampton instead of getting a good, steady job so she could save some money while she could – and then of course who felt totally vindicated when her errant daughter's uncouth boyfriend, with his uncombed black curls and diamond earring and Led Zeppelin T-shirts, refused to marry a pregnant Odette. And the arrest was, of course, the last straw. Matt's character in her mother's book was forever blackened.

Oh, Matt. Odette aches, suddenly: a physical spasm. An image of him which she tries to avoid, which is surely clichéd, but which recurs relentlessly, is imprinted beneath her half-closed eyelids: Matt seated on a grey-blanketed bed in a room empty except for the bed and a metal bucket: Matt with his curls greasy, his blue eyes lack-lustre, his earring removed.

I should have given in, she thinks. *I should have let him…*but she shudders violently, involuntarily, as if she has swallowed a fly, or moth. *I couldn't*, she thinks; *I couldn't. If I had known what he would do to Matt, if I had known he would steal six months of Matt's life, steal him away for six months from his son, from me – even then I don't know if I could have let him. Or whether I should have let him…*

She opens her eyes, suddenly. Mustn't worry about it, she thinks. Matt doesn't blame me – he said that. Although I don't know that for sure. He doesn't know about the other time. I couldn't tell him – couldn't. If I'd told him – how would he have reacted? I couldn't, oh I couldn't bear it if he'd said, *'Slut.'* Because sometimes, in Rockhampton, in Biloela, that's how men think. They think women are like men. They think, secretly, that a woman would *enjoy* it. *Enjoy* the forcing, the humiliation, the pain, the… Oh, shit. Shit. Don't go down that track again. Don't think about it. Think about something else.

What I'm going to do, when I get back: move back in with Julie in Rockhampton again, probably. If she doesn't mind having a baby in the flat. Julie, who since we first became friends in grade ten Mum disapproved of, saying she'd be pregnant as soon as put her bleached head out the door. What a laugh. She's far too wise and cautious for that. Unlike me. Fool, foolish, naive me…

Do some more subjects part-time? Go on a single mother's pension? What about if this works, and Matt gets out? Would I want to live with him – *could* I live with him – would he want to live with me?

Him, and his wild friends, the parties – he wouldn't give those up. Not yet. Not after what he'll have been through. It'd be a hell of a life for a child. For me. And yet, yet, I want him so badly. Just him, him. For me and Jason. Just for a while, even. He's Jason's father. Children need fathers. *I* need Matt, for me too. It's so hard on my own: too hard. All the worry, the decisions, the lack of sleep. Lack of love. Yes, maybe that's it. I need him to love me. And Jason. But I don't know if *he* loves *us*: either of us.

There are tears on her cheeks; she wipes her face quickly. She thinks, I'm just morbid because of the wine. I've got to be more rational, more logical. She takes a deep breath and blows her nose. What I need, really – of course! – is to move in with another mother. That's the sort of support I need: someone to compare notes with, advice with. And the children could play together. I don't need a nuclear family. At all. I've had enough experience of a nuclear family to last this lifetime…

She closes her eyes once more and holds her face taut. When she focuses again on the outside world, she is looking at her diary. She still hasn't written a word. Fleetingly, she thinks, I should write this down. But no. The book is for escape, for her sanity: to help her see that there are other ways of perceiving her world…

So, now, she is in France, in a warm, Christmas-scented van, and outside there is snow. Real snow. And somewhere a bell chiming, under a heavy, darkening sky.

She raises her pen. *I am outside the little village of Checy*, she writes.

*

Snow falls like flowers on her hood as Megan starts up the path to the telephone booth near the village. It's four o'clock and the sun has set, leaving the air bathed in a grey light which the snow makes luminous and shifting. Her boots slip a little on the frosted path and the lamps alongside her glimmer mistily.

In the fluorescent light of the booth, she fumbles in her backpack for her address book. She flips pages clumsily, until she finds 'D'. She takes a deep breath because her heart has begun to thump. She props the book open, under the weight of a phone directory, stares at the phone number printed under the address in the book, then tips coins from her purse into her gloved palm.

4

The Castle

It was August, the end of summer. They had travelled for three hours into the Massif Central, and by the time they arrived at the turn-off for the castle, Megan was ready to scream with irritation. Jean-Claude had curled himself into his habitual cocoon of spider legs and arms and glaring, bespeckled eyes; Isabelle was slumped away from Megan, thumb in her mouth, her limbs languid and supine; Alexandre, unrestrained as all in the back were, was bouncing his bowed legs on Megan's thighs, his two-year-old voice squealing excitedly, his hands clutching his parents' headrests and the incidental locks of hair resting on them.

'Aie! Mais arrête, Alexandre!' M. Ravel jerked his balding, bullet-head forward, to peer through his bifocals at the strip of gravel winding up the cliff; the plump, bejewelled hand of his wife patted his thigh appeasingly.

And then the castle came into view, its four lead-silver turrets perched like hats on watchful witches, its sandstone walls smooth and rosy pink in the afternoon light. They pulled off the road onto a grass track, drove past chicken coops, quiet and scented with domesticity, past a tethered black and white goat, whose yellow eyes cocked luridly at them over chewing lips, past a terrace of vineyards, fruiting, with leaves as pale green as fresh celery…towards a boy, waiting beside the path. Oh, save me, thought Megan, glimpsing him under Alexandre's jiggling elbows. Don't tell me this is the company they promised me. Because at that moment he looked just like a dog, a shaggy, lean dog, with silky hair falling over its face, and a whippet-like body, curved as it was over the gate he held open for them; just like a dog, until he stood upright, quite tall, and shook back the hair, and light eyes flashed, eyes too light to be a dog's, and too wide-set in a heart-shaped, spotted, hair-less face; but then he waved and smiled, and his mouth was broad and grinning and as eager to please as a puppy's, and Megan groaned and closed her eyes.

*

The car stopped, and the six of them tumbled out of the silver Citroen and stood, grouped and suddenly speechless in the quiet, slanting sun-light and the soft pink scent of age and earth billowing around them from the walls of the ghost-pale mansion. In her peripheral vision, Megan watched the boy swing the gate shut; then she turned to look with the others out over the acres of undulating valley falling away from the castle, and at the soft hills rising on the other side, cleared and ter-raced in places, leaving ridges like badly shaved patches on the skin of a woolly sheep. Amongst the terraces small stone buildings huddled against the hillsides, as camouflaged against the brown earth as caves.

But the silence was short-lived; with a shriek, the Lagrange family descended on them. Megan was swept after the Ravels into the cool darkness of twenfth-century stone, into a cool, open room with a flagged floor and narrow, four-paned windows set in metre-thick, broad alcoves. The walls were painted cream; near a vast dining table was a fireplace; against a wall was a candy-striped chaise longue.

'Oh, là, là, comme tu te grande!'

'Mais, qu'est-ce que tu t'as faite aux cheveux?'

'C'est Alexandre? Ça, c'est Alexandre? C'est pas vrai!'

Megan stood awkwardly, looking down, her shoulders with their slight stoop more pronounced than usual, her blonde bobbed hair falling to obscure her profile, holding Alexandre's nappy bag and one of the suitcases she'd pulled from the boot of the car while the children, six of them altogether, milled around the exclaiming adults with shrieks of fear or delight. Everyone ignored her, except the shaggy boy, who, she saw with exasperation, lolled in the streaming afternoon-lit doorway with his hair like a halo around his face.

31

'*Vous voulez que je monte avec les baggages?*' she said stiffly then to Madame Ravel.

'*Oui. Oui – Louis – où est-ce qu'on met les enfants? En haut?*'

'I'll take you up,' said the boy in the doorway, in a guttural English tinged with an American drawl.

Megan looked at him in surprise.

He picked up two duffel bags decorated with Disney characters and sauntered across the room to the staircase. 'These belong to Isabelle and Jean-Claude? Come with me. I'll show you to your room as well.' Like the Pied Piper, he began to mount the steps with the children jostling behind him.

Megan hesitated, then dropped the nappy bag, picked up the rest of Isabelle and Jean-Claude's things, found her own luggage, and followed them.

*

'You are to sleep here,' he said, smiling, placing on the bed one of the bags he had taken from her after they had organised the children. 'It's romantic, isn't it?'

And indeed it was. A turret room, circular, with a deep-set, narrow window, a single bed covered with a white counterpane, and a round table bearing a candlestick in a brass holder.

'You can see the sun spread over the mountain in the morning from here. It was my room for some holidays, since my stepbrothers and sister were born. Now I like the other tower, for a change. This is a good room, but too far up for the children. They all like to sleep near the parents, and they have fear of ghosts.' He stumbled throatily over the last word, and smiled, shrugging. 'Is that how it is said?'

'Near enough. Do you learn English at school?'

'Everyone does. We all want to go to America. Is that where you are from?'

'No, Australia. Have you heard of it?' She turned from him to the window and gazed out at the golden still light illuminating the valley.

She was conscious of his surprising height behind her and of his too-audible breath, and at the same time of the rising echoes from the children in the rooms a spiral of the stone staircase below.

'*Australie?* Of course. How could I have not?'

She shrugged, still facing the window. 'I went to America with the Ravels at Easter time. I went out to a bar with another au pair one night – she was French. A bloke trying to pick us up heard us speaking French, asked where I was from, and when I said Australia he said, "Do they speak French there?" Since then, I reserve my assumptions about the level of geographical education mainstream western countries promote.' She turned to look at him then, her hands behind her back, her chin lifted.

And he looked back, his head a little tilted with the blond fringe in disarming strands across one eye and an acned cheek, a frown lengthening his bottom lip. 'I'm sorry – you speak too fast – I –'

And she suddenly softened towards him. Living with the Ravels had taught her about the power of speaking one's native language: how quickly those who cannot express themselves fluently in a foreign language are at a disadvantage to the native speakers of that language; how humiliating it is to fumble for words and flounder in expression or comprehension. *Je m'excuse. Je suis fatigée, et j'ai faim.*' I'm tired and hungry, the excuses children use, or which are used to excuse children.

'Ah!' His eyebrows lifted and his eyes glinted.

'And I usually have the afternoon off from the children…to recover before the horror stretch.'

'The 'orror stretch?'

'Never mind. Can you show me where the bathroom is?'

'Oh – yes.' He looked suddenly embarrassed.

'Jesus.' Megan flicked her forehead in the French gesture, then under his puzzled gaze threw open the case he had placed for her on the bed and rummaged in it. 'How old are you?'

'Eighteen. And you?'

'Twenty.' She pulled out a small glass and a bottle of cognac triumphantly. 'I have one or two nips of this lately, while I have my afternoon bath. Helps me cope with the fam– with everything. Since I'm not getting a break today and surely not a bath until the kiddies are asleep I'll have one now. Join me?'

'Me? No! I mean, I don't drink spirits – wine with dinner yes –'

And then she thought, oh God, what if he tells them? What if he tells them that I've had a drink to cope with their children? But I'm leaving in a month. I can cope with their disapproval for that long. I've coped with everything else for five months, and the end is nigh...

'Ah, beautiful. So smooth. You're crazy, not drinking this stuff. After all, your race are the ones who perfected it. Okay. Well. How about you let me go to the loo and then you show us around the place? The kids need a run around. They've been cooped up for far too long. And there's miles of running space out there...'

She was over by the window again, drawn to it like a bubble to the surface of a pool. It was the focus of the room, as a switched-on television set is, even in a lounge room full of people; and it stopped her having to make too much real contact with the boy, Luc.

*

Megan found the two mothers in the castle's huge kitchen, rolling out dough. 'Luc's going to show us around: we'll take all the children,' she said, in English – then shook herself in surprise. Perhaps it was the cognac which had made her slip up, or the relief of speaking English to Luc after five months of trying not to.

She repeated the message in French, and watched the mothers exchange a smiling glance. Oh, God, she thought in disgust; they're trying to set me up with him! I can just see what they're thinking: Megan and Luc will flirt with each other, maybe even get it off, and everyone will be happy. She'll stop fretting from boredom and he'll enjoy his holiday with his half-siblings and they'll both look after the children. How sweet. We can just see them tripping through the flowers, rolling on the grass with the children, all of them laughing and giggling and tumbling over each other...

But he looked, when she caught up with them on the road down to the valley, quite happy enough with the children: the two elder boys swung on his forearms and Alexandre was chattering away in the stroller Isabelle pushed; the two other children wove around him, trying to catch his attention. He seemed quite oblivious to her approach.

*

For once, Megan was to eat with the adults. In the Ravels' home on the outskirts of Paris, she had always eaten with the children – so much for au pair meaning on an equal footing with the parents, she had often thought bitterly there. Not that she really wanted the company of the rotund couple, with Mme Ravel's family-centred, foolish conversation and M. Ravel's erratic, nervous outbursts. Of course, there had been a time, mainly on the long flight from Brisbane to Paris, that she had fantasised about them being quite different – about Mme Ravel being like Megan's mother had been – graceful and slim and gentle, a French-woman herself... But there could not have been a more vivid contrast.

But that first night in the castle, and then all subsequent nights in it, Mme Lagrange and Mme Ravel helped her bath, feed and settle at least the younger children, while the men drank aperitifs in the rosy seven o'clock light and made sure the casseroles or pies in the oven didn't burn, and Luc was off somewhere on his own. At eight thirty, while reading a final story by fluorescent torch to the two elder boys (and knowing very well that as soon as she left the room they'd be up to mis-chief), she was summoned to dinner.

The room was swimming with firelight: from the fireplace and from candles. The recesses of the windows, in daylight broad and open as the arms of a Madonna, in this light flickered with shadows and seemed to throw up their hands at some nameless indiscretion. The table was cov-ered with a white cloth, and a candelabra was placed at either end of it. Between the six candles, the four adults were animated, lifting glasses, forking olives and salami and sliced tomatoes, talking over one another. Luc was sitting quietly, at the far end of the table, leaning back in his chair, looking, to her surprise, almost sulky. His lip bottom drooped, as did his eyes. She looked at him longer than she had intended, therefore, so that he caught her eye as she descended the staircase; and he moved her then, through that first unguarded expression, with a strange little twist of sympathy.

She helped the women distribute plates, bring out courses, clear plates. M. Ravel, in an expansive mood, his bald pate and spectacles glistening in the candlelight, filled her wine glass twice. She listened to the adults talk – the women comparing children and schools and recipes, the men talking over them about soccer or the stock market – answered sudden questions about Australia from the Lagranges, stifled a yawn after the salad.

There was no real effort to include her or Luc in the conversation, despite their being asked to dine as adults; only M. Lagrange showed any real interest in Megan's replies to questions, but his bird-like wife was quick to distract him away from any dialogue with Megan which threatened to be even vaguely non-superficial. It was after Megan had observed this ploy at work a number of times that she understood: Mme Lagrange thought of her as a servant. It was a revelation, and not a pretty one. The Ravels themselves did not think of her as such, she was sure – they respected her student status, for one thing – but Megan had long ago learned that they were only really interested in themselves, their children, food and money-making.

She found herself wishing they had seated her nearer the equally stifled, for whatever reason, Luc. Once or twice, she caught him watching her.

After the cheese, she excused herself, saying she would start clearing up the kitchen. Start, she thought grimly; if I do it all, they'll expect me to every night, and I'll be damned before I'll become the kitchen-hand as well as everything else.

The castle was not connected to electricity, but there was a good strong lantern in the kitchen and a gas-powered hot water system and stove. Megan began rinsing dishes and stacking them on the worn timber bench beside the stone sink, collecting the cold foods in a basket, as she had been instructed, so they could be taken later down to the cellar, and stowing the flours and spices and herbs and sauces in the pantry.

As she was drying her hands, Luc came around the heavy oak door, carrying empty bottles.

'*Maman* wants me to get some more wine from the cellar. I'll take the basket down if you like.'

'I had no intention of taking it down,' said Megan, frowning. 'I've done my bit. I was going to go out for a walk now, actually. Have some time to myself.' Then she bit her lip, because his mouth had slipped again into its sulky droop. 'Come with me, if you like,' she said quickly, before she could change her mind, 'if you don't mind if I have a cigarette.'

How transparent he is, she thought, how really like a dog or a child. She couldn't help smiling at his mumbled 'Okay. Give me a moment,' and his quick exit down the steps to the cellar with the basket.

'I'll go up and get my coat. Meet you out the back,' she called after him.

*

The mountain was bathed in a three-quarter moon. Megan looked up at the castle, up at her dark turret, and at the boys' window behind which a pale light still flickered. They're still awake, she thought; but they were not her worry. Five hours a day of childcare, her contract had said. It had been more like ten. With housework and washing nappies thrown in for good measure. All for $80 a month, plus board and lodging. Oh, but let's not forget the trip to America, juggling hyperactive Jean-Claude and two-year-old, inquisitive Alexandre on a transatlantic flight complete with jet-lag at the end; and this one to the Massif Central, where she was expected to look after three others as well... All in the name of becoming fluent in a language which in all likelihood she would never be able to use in a country pandering more and more to the Japanese.

No – that was not quite honest. In the name, too, of a quest for a past, a sense of history, of belonging perhaps...and there was this. A twelfth-century castle and a rambling red rose winding around stone columns and a medieval valley whispering in moonlight.

'*On y va?*'

'Yes. Let's go.' Megan turned to Luc, who had come up silently behind her; and they began to walk side by side, solemnly, both with their hands in their pockets.

5

The Mountain

They walked in silence for a while, following a moon-whitened track down to a terraced vineyard. There was no sound except the occasional rustle of animal life in the grasses or shrubs or trees they passed. The air was cold, the mountain being high but still.

Eventually Megan said, 'How long has your family owned this place?'

'It's my mother's, and her parents' before that. Once, it was like a village – I'll show you tomorrow, if you like, the rooms for the footmen and maids the…men who worked with the horses.'

'The stable hands?'

'Yes. And all the old machines for making butter and cider and putting in and cutting crops are still here. My mother and stepfather think World War III is going to happen before the end of this century, so they're learning how to use everything, and trying to make it so they can…could…survive here without help from the outside world if necessary.'

'What do you think of that?'

He paused, and broke off a bramble strand which had caught the sleeve of his long pullover. 'I think if there is a World War III, there won't be any need for this place.'

'Yes, I agree.'

'But it's a nice place for a holiday. My half-brothers and sisters like it very much – the chickens, the goat, picking…cassis.'

'Blackberries. Yes, I saw that this afternoon. I'm not sure the chickens like them so much. The goat can hold her own.'

He shrugged. 'They are children.'

'So everybody keeps saying. Mind if we sit down for a minute so I can have a cigarette?'

'There's a place a little further which is nice to sit. You can see the stream from there.'

They could hear it before seeing it: a musical trickle of water, light and fresh in the night air. Luc led the way off the path to a broad, flat stone from which the hill dropped steeply for about two hundred metres. Way down, Megan glimpsed the spangle of moonlight on the moving water; above the hills was the vast expanse of sky: black velvet studded with the silver points of pins.

'Do you want one?'

'No, thank you. They're bad for your health, you know.' He sat cross-legged on the stone and Megan dropped beside him, wrapping her arms around her knees.

'Oh, I know. I'll give them up when I'm old enough.'

She looked at him curiously as she pocketed the rest of the cigarettes and matches. He was eighteen, yet he seemed to have no desire to test the taboos of childhood life. Perhaps, she thought, the rites of passage were different for the French. Certainly they drank table wine from quite a young age. Or perhaps it was just him.

'So, you're still at school, you said.'

'Yes. At *collège*. Next year, I will begin my military service.'

'Military service? You're kidding.' She blew out a long stream of smoke, which drifted whitely out over the valley.

'No. It's necessary here.'

'Compulsory, you mean? The government says you have to do it?'

'Yes. But necessary, as well.'

Megan was tempted to say, oh you're indoctrinated well, but refrained. His eyes were large and soft in the cloudless night; his eyelashes dropped shadows over his cheeks when he had finished speaking as if to sweep away her criticism.

So there was a sudden silence. Megan waited, conscious of a rising, habitual irritation she had had before with boys who could only talk about themselves, who made no effort to engage a girl in conversation she might find interesting. But are there any other types of boys? she thought, jiggling a foot furiously. Why the hell should we find any of them interesting, if it wasn't for…what? Sex? Conquest? A desire to give, or to receive, contact, affection, love?

'You don't have military service in Australia?'

She jerked her head up and drew on the cigarette sharply. 'No way.'

Another silence threatened, so she said quickly, half-angrily, 'I went to a very posh school in Australia, to do my last two years of school. Won a scholarship there. A boarding school. Wanted to get away from Dad's new family – my mother's dead, you see. Died when I was twelve. Hated that school, though: the arrogance of the rich.'

He was looking at her, frowning, concentrating on following her English. He started to say, 'I'm sorry – did you say your mother is…' but she cut him off quickly.

'Then I started at uni last year. Doing Arts. French and Journalism and Fine Arts. I'll go back next year.'

'Fine Arts?'

'Yes – studying paintings. Learning about art and artists. My two objectives in coming here, to Europe, this year were to improve my French and see lots of paintings in the original.' And to experience something of my mother's past, she thought, but didn't say. 'Dad put up the money for it. Thought it would do me good.'

'It seems a strange combination, the three.'

'Not really. With French, I might to able to eventually get into the Diplomatic Corps, or get posted somewhere to be a correspondent, and painting's about creating images of particular times and places, I think, which articles often do too. And analysing events, impressions. Anyway, that's the plan. Whether I'll get a job when I'm finished is another matter.' She stubbed out her cigarette on the smooth surface of the stone and slipped the butt automatically into the pocket of her coat. 'So what's your plan after military service?' Here I go again, she thought, getting him to talk about himself. How well trained I've become in getting boys to talk about what interests them! But she recognised too, grudgingly, her own defensiveness: her own way of avoiding disturbing sympathy.

'I have no idea.'

'Really? Oh, come on, you must have some idea – favourite subjects, things you're good at...'

'No, I don't know. I have made no plans. Perhaps I will care for this place for a while, just live here and care for the animals and crops, write some poems perhaps.'

Megan looked at him sideways and saw that he was half-smiling, but dreamily, looking out over the valley, over its ribbed terraces and pale sandstone dwellings and dark woolly trees, and over the bright tinkle of the stream below. She said nothing.

'After all,' he continued suddenly, turning to look at her, 'people have done it for hundreds – thousands – of years. It is my mother's and she pays someone to care for it when they are not here. Why not pay me instead?'

'Why not?' said Megan lightly, remembering his quietude at dinner and remembering too, suddenly, his mother's rather brisk requests of Luc to fetch this, fetch that. She continued gently, 'Except that it's a bit escapist, don't you think? Not really living in the twentieth century? And wouldn't you be bored with it, after a time?'

'Perhaps. Perhaps. But I like the thought of it. The twentieth century is not such a nice place to live, in any case.' He was staring out at the valley, not at her.

'Better than any other, in many ways, I would have thought. And it is our century, after all. We have a duty to it, don't you think? To do what we can to solve its problems?'

He smiled faintly, then, and inclined his head to her; he caught her eye and held it. 'That's a very romantic idea,' he said, and his face relaxed suddenly into the broad, infectious grin he had worn as he had swung the gate open that afternoon; and so made Megan laugh, a high, unexpectedly happy sound which startled a bird from the undergrowth beside them.

The castle was in darkness when they came back to it, but unlocked. 'You know your way?' asked Luc softly.

Megan could barely make out his shape, so complete was the blackness inside once the door was shut. 'I think so,' she whispered, 'if I can find the stairs…'

'Here.'

Megan felt her hand groped for and caught; his fingers, cold, smooth, bony, gripped hers awkwardly.

'There are candles over here – wait.'

A match was struck: their shadows sprang hugely on the stone walls.

'*Voilà.* You remember the way to your room?'

'Yes. Thank you. Well, good night then.' She looked back at him, but he was busy adjusting his own candle in its brass holder.

'Okay. *Bonne nuit.*'

He followed her, at an awkwardly close distance, since neither spoke again, until the darkness swallowed him at the turn to the northern turret; Megan started up the final flight of steps to her room with a heart beating faster from not only the exertion of the climb.

*

All the next morning, Megan was occupied with the younger children: helping them dress and eat, making their beds, sorting out their squabbles, clearing up their mess. Alexandre, being only two, was the most difficult, but the Lagrange three-year-old, Pierre-Michel, proved a handful as well. Megan cared for them automatically, instinctively; without real affection, except occasionally for Alexandre. Changing Alexandre's nappy, turning her face away from the stench and holding his squirming torso and legs firmly with one forearm while she swabbed his bottom with soaked cotton wool, she thought, how foolish the nanny system is: how absurd to expect a total stranger to give a child the unselfish care it needs just because it is a child, or for the child to return any real affection, when the nanny changed faces every six months. The one of course who lost out the most was the child: the parents had relief, the nanny learned the language – the child simply learned to cope. Usually badly.

But although she was fully occupied through the morning, she was still conscious of intermittent guitar chords sounding from the northern turret, and of Luc's descent at last, and disappearance with the older children down the track leading to the goat and chickens.

*

'Il n'y a plus de lait,' said Mme Ravel at eleven o'clock. *'May-gun, tu peux aller à la ferme?'*

Anything, Megan thought, for a respite from the babies. She had volunteered early in her stay with the Ravels to run errands when they needed something – bread, or lettuce, or milk, as now – provided she could go alone. They had eventually stopped asking her to take a couple of the children along for the ride, or walk.

The farm where she was instructed to buy milk was four kilometres away, so she took the Citroën. And so passed Luc, returning from the chicken coop with the older children and a basket of eggs.

'Where are you going?' he asked, leaning in the passenger window. She told him.

'Good, I'll come with you. I want some hay for the vegetable garden and the chickens.' He turned to the children, Jean-Claude, Isabelle, Paul and Eugenie, spoke to them rapidly, watched them start reluctantly toward the house, then climbed in beside Megan. 'Are you having a nice day?' he asked in his polite, American-tinged accent.

'Okay,' she said carefully.

'Pierre-Michel is difficult sometimes. He's the baby; he's…*gaté.'*

'Spoilt?'

'Yes.'

'Well…they don't have many things to play with here. And I have to watch them all the time, with the stairs and things: there's that break

44

in the wall on the mountain side where they could fall down the hill if they weren't careful.'

She was aware of his body curled against the car door, his knees toward her; his fringe was pushed off his face for once and his eyes had dropped to her thigh, perhaps unconsciously. Her legs were bare, tanned: the day was sunny and warm; and her skirt was rucked up from the movement of entering the car. She didn't straighten the skirt.

'You're good with them.'

She shrugged. 'Mediocre.'

'And there are no paintings around here for you to look at, in your time off.'

She smiled at him, and his eyes smiled back, holding her gaze: and his expression made her heart lurch, and then spread a heat across her chest, her throat and her cheeks. His pupils were large and the irises startlingly blue, like the pale blue packed powder in a child's paintbox, she thought suddenly. Then he moved his head and the fringe of hair broke across his vision, and she looked back at the road.

'If there were, they'd all be of a quietly suffering Christ, I imagine. If it was pre-Renaissance stuff.' She kept her voice deliberately off-hand.

'You're a not a Christian?'

'Used to be. Now I don't know what I believe in. Fate, destiny, perhaps. Everything has already happened: the future's as unchangeable as the past. It's easier that way. What about you?' She glanced at him again, and saw that his whole body was turned to her, and that he was watching her face.

'Oh, yes, I believe in God. Christian laws – the Ten Commandments – are the basis of our laws anyway.'

'Not all of them.'

'Which are not?'

'Well, "Thou shalt honour the Lord thy God", "Thou shalt not have false idols before you" for a start.' She took the bends in the mountain road carefully.

'Yes…okay.'

'And what about "Thou shalt not covet thy neighbour's goods." "Thou shalt not covet thy neighbour's wife"?'

'Desire is the beginning of the sin. It is wise to recognise that.'

Well, thought Megan, seeing in her peripheral vision that his eyes were lowered to her legs: it looks to me as if you're coveting me; but then I'm no one's goods or wife.

But of course she did not say that.

6

Turrets

How strange it was, Megan thought, lying in her turret room with her candle extinguished and moonlight like a patch of white paper on the worn timber floor, that the focus of her mind could change so completely in just twenty-four hours. Was it like this with everyone, that a rational, sober, bored but conscientious brain could be obscured so swiftly by…what was it? Desire? That now, instead of reading, or thinking about the past or the future, or sleeping, she could think only of the cool bony softness of his hand on her hand in the darkness, or his eyes on her thigh. She could not even clearly remember his face when she tried to conjure it up: only the clear blue flash of his eye, the slight hook of his nose in profile, the rash of spots on his cheek, the fall of shaggy hair. An immature, unpolished face, beautiful because it was young and vulnerable, perhaps. A face she could imagine touching with her lips, gently, breathing moth-wing flutters over its surface.

Alive, she thought, I am alive again. Because her body under the cotton cocoon of her bed sheets had begun to tingle: as if it had been sleeping these past five months, and now was rippled by some unseen current, as a moth when perfectly developed in a chrysalis is rippled to awake and emerge, imago – her sexuality unfurled suddenly, completely, overnight almost, from the sleeping pupa it had curled itself into under the pseudo-parental influence of the Ravels and the intimidation of a foreign country and foreign language.

She slipped her legs from under the sheet and sat on the edge of the bed. She was naked. She flexed a calf in the square of moonlight. The muscle was smooth, shaved; it bulged like a breast. Had that struck him in the car as he watched her legs? she wondered. She stretched out her hands on her thighs: the fingers were fine and strong and competent. As she had driven and talked, her hands firm on the wheel and the gearstick, had he been listening to her, or only partly listening – had he been thinking about brown thighs on white cotton sheets and a glare of summer light angling through a turret window, and her hands on his body, and his on hers?

She ran her hands over her hips and up to her breasts. Had he looked at the curve of her breasts under her T-shirt as her shoulders tensed to swing the wheel, at the tilt of her chin and the arc of her cheek? If she had not acted normally, ignoring the impulse to hold his gaze, to swim in his dense blue irises and their dilated centres, if she had not stared through the windscreen when he spoke to her; if she had smiled into his eyes more, held longer contact, dropped her eyes to his shorts, what might have happened? When they arrived at the farm gate, and she parked the car under a tree and turned off the ignition, would there have been a silence, would both of them have found their hearts pumping unnaturally: what now? what now?

An intake of breath if she'd touched his cheek, a wide-eyed silence as they adjusted, a tremulous second suspended…then her gasp as his head came at her and his lips groped her face and stumbled over her cheek and found her mouth and she peeled back his shirt and pressed her breasts into his skin…smooth, warm, his heart vibrating…his arms drawing around her, the relief of falling into him, into his skin with its sheen of desire, into the cocoon of his breath, of his tall beauty and warmth, of his hands groping and his mouth hungry, urgent, eating her, her face and neck, her throat, finding her…

Oh stop it, she thought, stop! As if, as if! He was a child, undoubtedly a virgin; it would never happen that way: it would be clumsy and awkward and ultimately unsatisfying, at least for her. And how could she indulge in such trash, such fantasy, anyway? It was vain and unreal and Cinderella-scarred thinking, and she was a fool and an idiot and a pathetic product of conditioning to even imagine that it might. She saw herself as the prize, rather that the winner: she thought about him undressing her, rather than undressing him: she wanted not to own, but to be owned. Pathetic.

She swung her legs back under the sheets, straightened the counterpane and turned herself on her side. Pathetic.

*

The days that followed – almost a week and a half of them – settled into a routine. Megan occupied herself with the children in the morning; Luc emerged late; both she and Luc ate the midday meal with the children. After lunch, while the younger children slept, Megan was given two hours off, which she used to read, or write careful letters to her father, and have a quiet bath afterwards.

In the afternoons, she and sometimes Luc followed the children around the mountain, picking berries, or exploring the stone ruins, or pushing go-carts on the dirt tracks, or fetching bread or milk from the farms. Then she helped bath the children, feed them and put them to bed; she would afterwards eat with the adults and Luc, help with the clearing up, and in the late evenings go out for a stroll. Sometimes, Luc would accompany her, sometimes not – so every night when she excused herself to stack and clear in the kitchen, she would wait in agitated suspense for him to follow her, or not.

And there lay the difference for Megan between the first two days and the subsequent ones. Because despite her self-berating that second night, her mind swung to Luc like a compass to a pole: she was aware of wherever he was; she could not look at him without a flutter of her nerves; everything she said to him (which seemed suddenly little) sounded artificial or strained. She shook herself angrily, impatient with the juvenile mess into which she had deteriorated; at the same time thrilling at the sexual electricity even verbal contact with him sparked through her. In her bath, despite self-mockery, she went over and over his gestures and expressions, his responses to her, and over and over their conversations, particularly the occasional evening ones in which, away from the appraising eye of Luc's mother – Megan had been wrong, apparently, about her being as eager for Megan and Luc to get along as the Ravels had been; the woman seemed as possessive about her son as about her second husband – it seemed they both flirted quite openly. She studied her body in the mirror: if she stood up straight, instead of allowing her shoulders to hunch as she habitually did, her body looked firm and strong, the waist narrow and the breasts pleasantly full.

She chose what she wore with care. She no longer focused on the beauty of the mountain, of the colour of the air, of the crumbling medieval castle. She was, she thought meditatively as she read to Isabelle and Eugenie one night, as bewitched as a character in a French fairy tale.

*

One night at dinner, Luc was more animated than she had previously seen him. The conversation had turned to the self-sufficiency of the castle in terms of heating and food, and the improvements needed to it. She watched his face across the table in the candlelight: the stillness of his lips as he listened, the way he raised one eyebrow when he began to speak, the trick of light which faded to smoothness the planes below his cheekbones. His previous tension with his mother seemed to have vanished at last. His voice in French was less guttural, more musical, than in English, and very rapid, as if he thought he might be cut off before he could formulate into words what he wished to express.

Then, after two glasses of wine, she almost let her guard down: almost flirted with him in front of the adults. She bit back a teasing response to something he said just in time: and even so caught Mme Lagrange's suspicious eye. And so, as soon as there was a break in the conversation, Megan excused herself and ducked out into the kitchen with a pile of plates.

The trouble was, she thought, as she began mechanically to stack and rinse bowls and glasses, she really didn't know whether he was simply flirting with her, or whether he genuinely wanted her. He was too difficult to read, compared to Australian boys she had known. With them, at uni, it had been relatively simple: if there was mutual attraction, then they asked you out, and you moved from dating to touching hands to bed quite quickly; and when it ended, you had the pleasure of the memory, an added dimension to a particular time and place, and often a residual fondness; sometimes even a lasting friendship. Unless one of you fell in love badly, into that pit of desperate, desperate grief when the affair ended… As she had with David.

David. Was it because of him, because she had never fallen out of love with him, even when he left, kindly, quietly, saying they both had to move on, saying he was going to Sydney, that she should apply for a scholarship, she was certainly clever enough to win one, that he'd see her, of course, when they both came back on holiday – they lived beside each other, after all – was it because of him, her first love and lover, the first person to assuage some of the grief of losing her mother, that she carried this attitude to sex now? This concentration on a longing for physical union rather than spiritual? This reluctance, refusal even, to allow herself to dream of more than that again? Probably.

But even so, she had not been stunned with desire quite so swiftly before. It was probably the five months of celibacy which had triggered it, she thought, or his open friendliness, or attraction. Or perhaps it was his virginity: the very fact that his experiences were probably so different from her own, that she could teach him so much. Or the simple fact that he was French…

'Tu vas sortir ce soir?'

Megan jumped, startled. Luc placed the salad bowl and more plates on the timber bench beside her.

'Oh, yes, of course I'm going out! The moon is nearly full – it's so lovely…' She faced him, her eyebrows raised.

'Well, it's just…' Luc swept the hair from his face and looked at her sideways. 'I'm making a song. I can't finish it as I want it. I thought perhaps, when you come back from your walk, you might listen to it? Tell me what you think? My parents –' he shrugged, a quick half-grin flashing across his mouth and eyes – 'they don't approve. They wouldn't like it.'

'Oh, I'd love to hear it! I mean, I don't know how good a critic I'd be, but thank you. I'm flattered that you…trust me.' She felt the blood in her cheeks.

He shrugged again, smiling. 'See you later then. The north turret.'

She nodded, biting back the 'I know' which sprang to her lips.

*

The women were still in the kitchen, finishing the cleaning up, Megan supposed, when she returned from her stroll; the men had disappeared, probably to their individual pursuits. M. Ravel was a loner, a socially awkward man, only comfortable when his competent wife was with him to lift the burden of conversation from his sloping shoulders. He coped with pre-dinner conversation with M. LaGrange by drinking martinis, by roaming the room restlessly to refill their glasses whenever there was a lull in the talk, and because M. LaGrange was an easy-going, talkative host who could turn the state of his shoes into a half-hour topic for debate. But after-dinner conversation was a different matter; when the wine had run out and his belly was full, M. Ravel shuffled off to the bathroom and didn't return. And M. LaGrange probably breathed a sigh of relief and took his daily newspaper off to bed.

Megan lit a candle from the cluster kept in round brass holders on a table at the bottom of the staircase. She breathed deeply, trying to steady her heart. Then she mounted the smooth, stone steps, past the nasal breathing of the allergic Jean-Claude, past the silent bedroom of the little girls, past M. Ravel's snuffling snores. Her hand on her chest, she tapped lightly of Luc's door.

'*Entrez!*' He was sitting cross-legged on the single bed with his guitar.

The room was similarly furnished to her own, except that there was a desk and a bookcase against the wall and a worn single sofa near the window. A number of candles steeped the corners with ghostly shadows.

'Have a seat.' He indicated the sofa.

Megan obediently and thankfully dropped into it, pulling her knees up and wrapping her arms around them automatically.

'How was your walk?'

'Oh, lovely. The moon was quite stunning.' Was there a slight reprimand in her tone? Or a quiver of nervousness? Which would he pick up? 'Okay, well, let's hear it.' Her voice was rushed and breathless. She lowered her eyes. Concentrated.

Knowing the little she did about him, she was prepared for a protest song, a song belonging to the sixties: a song about nuclear disarmament and environmental damage and the destructive nature of cities. So she was genuinely surprised at the swift, staccato beat of the incomprehensible lyrics he ground out for her. When he finished, abruptly, flattening his strum hand across the guitar strings, and flicking his gaze to hers, his eyebrows raised expectantly, she could only stare back at him from her curled position, frozen.

'I'm sorr– I missed some words. I didn't quite get... I like the beat: it's very now, a bit like the Ramones, you know them? American semi-punk band? Might be better on an electric guitar. Have you got a copy of the lyrics?'

'An electric guitar? Of course, it would be better, but I only have this one. Yes, I have the lyrics here, on the bed.' He leaned across to her with a sheet of paper, his hair falling over half his face.

She accepted it without touching his hand. She held the paper to the light of a candle and glanced over it rapidly; then had to go back and read more slowly. Then she look up, puzzled. 'But this is just a description of "Place de la Gare", wherever that is. It's beautiful, a bit cynical – this bit about the soldiers fondling the babies to get round their nurses, for instance...'

He was looking at her intently, and she suddenly realised what she had said. She stumbled on, 'I expected a message song, I don't know why. A political song. But this is very unusual – I can see why you're having trouble finishing it. It's very poetic and insightful, but isn't going anywhere in particular, especially for a song. Maybe you need a chorus, some catchy lines repeated, and a bit of variety of rhythm, perhaps?' She was speaking too quickly, she knew, for him to follow her; she took a quick breath and repeated, 'You need a chorus, I think, and some variation in the rhythm. But it's very poetic – some great lines.'

He was quiet, looking at her. Then he said, 'Yes, you're right. Only, I wanted to try something different, more unusual…' He paused, still looking at her, or perhaps at the song inside his head.

'Oh, look, really, as I said, I know nothing about music…'

'No, perhaps you are right. There is a line I could repeat, only a line, so that the point is clearer…'

Megan sat silent and frozen under his meditative gaze – until she could stand it no longer. 'Do you have any others? I mean, I'm not much use, but if you'd like to play another…'

'Other songs?' He blinked and moved his head; the hair fell across his eye again. 'Yes – yes – I do, but – tomorrow perhaps? I would like to work with this one – thank you – it helps so much, you know, for someone to listen.' He smiled, radiantly, then.

'It's okay. Really, it was a pleasure.' She was standing up, smoothing her skirt, flicking her bobbed hair behind her ears. 'I liked it – it really is very poetic. Well, goodnight then.' She hesitated, her heart pounding. Give him time to make a move, you silly girl, she thought.

But it was too late. He stayed on the bed, looked up at her, smiling. *'Bonne nuit.'*

She closed the door behind her.

7

The Mistral

Megan woke suddenly at five thirty. Her window had banged shut: in her dream, it had been a door slamming in her face. Which door? And why? The frayed threads of dream memory clung to the jagged edge of reality: something to do with Australia, school, her father…

She stared at the square of light – oyster-silver, luminous – the turret window allowed into the room. A tree swayed across it in sepia-brown against a white sky. There was a wind whistling around the corners of the frame, catching in whipped gasps at the edges of the timber. She had had to pull up a blanket during the night. Perhaps this was the mistral she had heard about? A wind which blew in the Massif Central for three days at a time, or six, or nine. A wind invested with myth, with the magic of numbers, with almost religious significance.

She shook herself away from the dream, which nagged like a mosquito bite on the edge of her consciousness. There was no point in worrying about things past, about rejection, not here, not now. Not when there was a twist of hope in her throat when she thought of the night before, the day ahead, not when there were visions of possibility flitting like moths in her head, not when her limbs were being quietly rinsed with a slowly pumped adrenalin. Because the invitation to Luc's room, the song – surely they could mean only one thing?

'Luc,' she whispered. All she would have to do would be to pad quietly down her turret steps and up his, open his door, climb into his bed, while he was still sleeping… And they could live for the next week and a half in the sensual, altered world of the couple, live with a delicate, secret knowledge of each other in the everyday, ignorant land of the Family…

But what if, despite the invitation, despite the flirting, he did not want her? If he should be shocked instead of elated, reject her instead of embrace her, cry out, wake the families – slam the metaphorical door in her face… It was impossible. She could not do it.

She shuddered suddenly. Why did she desire him so? His face drifted behind her eyes. He was pale, cold-blooded, surely, with those cold fingers and anaemic skin, pimply, his nose in profile hooked. But soft-haired and sea-eyed and graceful in a long-limbed way. And he smiled at her as she had not been smiled at for a long, long time, it seemed; and he flirted with her and asked to be flirted with.

That was all. That was all. Not enough to base anything on.

She lay quietly for a moment, watching the light in her room thicken. Then, abruptly, she flipped back her covers and swung out of bed. She pulled on jeans and a sweater, opened her door and slipped down her turret steps. And hesitated. A crossroad. Despite her fear, despite her logic, it was still possible… Her heart beat with fright, as if she really had a choice, as if she could really choose one over the other. As if the fiction in her head could actually be realised.

She stepped down.

*

In the kitchen, she put the hexagonal coffee pot on the gas stove and rubbed her hands together over the rising heat. She looked absently out the deep-set window above the stove. Out in the valley, the wind was caught in the trees, so the leaves glittered in the first rays of the sun like hair ruffled by restless fingers strung with diamonds. A window of one of the castles across the valley flamed suddenly, like burning paper, as the sun caught the glass. The sky was a blue wash, onto which the sunrise had spilled pink powder.

There was a movement behind her, a scuffling sound. Her heart leapt. For one wild second, she thought… But no, it was Isabelle and Eugenie, huddled together, peeking around the kitchen door, their faces, Isabelle's fair and Eugenie's dark, both pointed-chinned and impish.

'What are you two doing up so early?' Megan asked in French. They usually stayed playing and giggling in their bedroom until the boys forced them out.

'We heard you come down.'

'The wind woke me up. Is it the mistral?'

'Yes. It brings luck – sometimes good, sometimes bad.'

The coffee pot began it bubble: Megan turned it down and poured a little milk into a pan.

Then she paused to look over her shoulder at the little girls, the carton still in her hand. 'Do you two want me to make you warm milk?'

Neither of the little girls had slippers on: they shivered together in their long nightdresses, dancing their feet on the cold flagstones.

'Can we have some coffee?' Isabelle's eyes slanted sideways at Megan, crafty as a vixen's.

Megan knew Mme Ravel, Isabelle's mother, had a *horreur* of caffeine for the children, believing it would immediately send them wild: in Jean-Claude's case, she probably had a point, but Isabelle had quite a mild temperament unless pushed to the limit by her older brother.

'Well, here's the deal: if you two go and dress yourselves in something warmer, I'll make you some milk coffee. But be very quiet – don't wake the boys!'

They scampered off, whispering, in league with Megan against the Boys. By the time they returned in jeans, bright jumpers and sneakers, Megan was spooning sugar into their weak brews. The three sat at the scrubbed kitchen table like conspirators, and sipped.

'Do you like it?'

'Mmm – it's good!'

'You mustn't tell the others, or your mothers: they might be cross with me.'

'Jean-Claude goes crazy when he has coffee. He sneaks it sometimes from someone's cup when they're not looking!'

'Boys,' said Megan, rolling her eyes in sympathy. 'They're a pain.'

'What about Luc?' Eugenie looked at Megan from under her lashes.

'Luc?'

'Do you like him?'

'Well, he's more of a man, really, than a boy. He's okay. It's nice to have some-one my own age to talk to.'

The little girls exchanged glances and smirked.

'Why? Do you think he likes me?' Megan's tone was carefully challenging.

But the two just giggled and buried their noses in their coffee bowls.

*

All morning, the wind whined around the castle, and by ten o'clock the children's need to burn off energy had reached desperation point. Mme Ravel, in a moment of inspiration, commissioned Megan to take all six of them on a walk down to the closest farm to buy eggs. Their own chickens had not been enough to cope with two families.

'I can't manage all of them on my own!' protested Megan, in her firmest French.

She was irritated by the wind, by the boisterous noise of the cooped-up boys, by the assumption that she should amuse all of the children, by the fact that Luc had still not emerged from his turret haven. He does not really like me, she had decided irritably. He wants me to listen to his songs and theories, massage his ego, but he won't give anything back. He's lazy and selfish. How could I have even thought of visiting his bed this morning?

Mme Lagrange stopped her search for boots and straightened: she looked at Megan with two fingers pressed against her lips.

'What if the elder ones run ahead to the main road?' Megan added, weakly.

'Yes,' she said after a moment's pause, 'it might be dangerous. Luc can go with you. Luc! Luc!' She turned abruptly and her voice was strident, giving her eldest son's name two syllables with the accent on the 'c', so it sounded like 'Lu-ka'.

There was no reply. Exasperated, Mme LaGrange threw up her

hands and started determinedly up the staircase. 'Look for that boot under the couch!' she called to Eugenie over her shoulder.

And by the time the children were dressed for the walk, Luc, his face creased from sleep and sheepishly tousled, had joined them.

The wind whipped pink into their cheeks and hair in lashing strands across Megan's face. They walked in the middle of the dirt track which wound down the mountain. The little girls skipped together, the elder boys switched at roadside brambles, Megan pushed Alexandre in his stroller and Luc carried his youngest half-brother, Pierre-Michel, on his shoulders.

For a while, Luc chattered to Pierre-Michel and Megan strode against the wind in silence. Only when Pierre-Michel grew restless and wriggled down to find a switch and copy the older boys did Luc turn with a lopsided smile to Megan.

'It's amazing how the mistral changes the temperature, isn't it?'

'Yes,' Megan replied in English to his English, her heart leaping, despite her resolution to be cold toward him. She continued in English partly to spite the children who would understand little of what they said, even if it would add no fuel to their gossip, and partly to have the advantage over Luc. 'I'd heard about it. They warned me to bring warm clothes.'

'It's nice, that sweater, very colourful. Did you buy it here, in France?'

'No – an old boyfriend in Australia gave it to me.' She tossed her head and glanced at him sideways, to gauge his reaction; but his head was in profile and she could read little of his expression.

'Australian wool is famous here,' Luc said blandly. 'But I thought Australia was very hot?'

'It still gets cold in winter. Especially in the south. It even snows down there sometimes. I do believe that sometimes you can even ski!' Megan's voice was threateningly innocent. 'We probably have our own version of the mistral in our mountains. It's just a wind, after all, *n'est-ce pas?*

59

'Well, it – ' Luc was frowning, rising to the bait '– it has many stories about it. Legends, I suppose.'

'There are Aboriginal stories about some of our winds too, I'm sure. But nobody believes those myths any more: we all know that the causes of wind are natural, not supernatural. We don't need myths to explain weather any more.'

'But the stories are still important, especially to children. French children love our stories.' He turned and smiled radiantly at her.

And suddenly her anger, her irritation, vanished.

'Yes, well, I suppose you're right. We have fairy stories in Australia too, you know.'

But, she thought, they were only children's bedtime stories, not really legends; perhaps she was so cynical about French stories like the mistral ones because she had no myths of her own, truly her own – the only legends twentieth-century white Australians told belonged to other cultures – Aboriginal, or European or American. And she had a sudden urge to say that to him, to say that it was the French stories and traditions which gave his culture its richness, and that was partly what she had come to France for – that her mother had been French and she longed to adopt her past, to belong to a history steeped in magic and drama and a way of living, that she was on a journey in search of such richness, a hopeless journey, because someone else's past could never be hers, but in the experiencing of taking part in it, however briefly, perhaps some of its peace might rub off like gold dust onto the rest of her life…

But Luc had been distracted by Pierre-Michel, who was calling to him to come and see a lizard or a butterfly or some other creeping creature, and the other children were already at the farm gate, swinging it open, and she had to push the stroller quickly to catch up because there were cows in the field, and they might be let out.

*

It was only on the return trek to the castle that Megan and Luc spoke directly to each other again. They had stored the purchased food in the stroller, since Alexandre had tired of being pushed and scampered now after the older children, who forged ahead. Luc had control of the stroller and Megan, gratified at this thoughtfulness, walked beside him.

'So,' he said, flashing his eyes at her, 'when do you go back?'

'To Australia?'

'No, I mean to Paris.'

'Oh – the end of next week.' She glanced at him quizzically. She had assumed he knew that. 'How about you?'

'Tomorrow I'm going down the mountain, with my stepfather. He has some business in Montpellier. He's a stockbroker, you know. He wants to teach me some things about that.'

Megan's heart contracted sharply. 'Oh, I thought –' she said before she could catch herself.

'Yes?' He had turned to look at her, only seemingly mild interest, or concentration on her English perhaps, on his face.

'I thought you were all on holiday,' she answered hurriedly.

'We are. But when the stocks change, you know... He, my stepfather, listens to the radio, follows it very carefully. They want to retire as soon as they can so they can live here. He wants me to look after the shares when I'm older.' Was there apology in his voice?

'It's – probably a great thing to learn.' She's looking at him sideways.

'Will you be all right with the children while I'm gone?'

She crumpled then, all her self-control dissipating: he sounded so much like a husband, and such a deluded one at that: she doubled over, holding her diaphragm, laughing so much she could barely breath.

He stopped pushing the stroller and watched her, straight-faced.

She managed to gasp out at last, 'How long will you be gone?' then collapsed hysterically again at her own wifeliness.

'A few days. What's so funny?' He really didn't understand.

After a moment, he began to push the stroller again, his back slightly offended; she stumbled after him, mopping her eyes on the

sleeve of her jumper. Oh, she thought, you need to learn so much –
when you come back, when you come back, I will, I will, go to your
bedroom!

8

Courage

While Luc and his father were gone, the mistral died.

*

All right, Megan thought, the afternoon they arrived back. Pollen was as thick as mist in the still air of the valley and sunlight hung in it like Spanish moss. All right, she thought, watching their car swing into the driveway and park beside a bramble rose spilling blossoms as red as the blood pounding in her chest. What have I got to lose? His friendship perhaps – a week of friendship – and he'd still have to have contact with me, should surely see it as flattering, not find me offensive, surely… And to gain? A week of bliss, of heightened life, of satisfied desire, of affirmation and, perhaps, perhaps, continued connection in Paris…?

All right, she thought. Tonight.

*

Before dinner, she stood in the bathroom and looked at herself in the mirror by candlelight. Her eyes were dark and huge and frightened, her mouth tense. She unbuttoned her blouse slowly. She unclipped her bra and removed it. She cupped her breasts in her hands. They were full, hard-nippled, translucently white in the flickering light.

She put her blouse back on and took the bra up to her turret room. She poured herself a glass of cognac. She remembered his open smile and wave as he had emerged from the car. She remembered him holding her eye contact as they walked toward each other on the stairs, he coming down, she going up – the vividness of his blue-crystal irises and the

63

darkness of his pupils and the slant of his lashes. She remembered him walking with her and the children to feed the farm animals, smiling at her, looking at her fully, easily, his gaze dropping down her body when he finished something he was saying.

She thought of their naked bodies facing each other, then slowly touching, fingertip to fingertip, hair-end to hair-end, lip to lip, neck to neck, breast to chest, hip brushing hip – and then the urgency, the urgency underneath...

She put her hands to her cheeks and felt them burning hot, and her arms heavy with pulsing blood.

*

After the main course, she rose quickly and excused herself. She rinsed plates with nervous fingers. Would he follow her? If he did not, she resolved, she would just go to bed and leave it at that. She wiped the benches automatically and efficiently, her movements brisk and agitated. Why couldn't M. Ravel have been more liberal with the wine he'd poured her? It would have helped with this...*terror*, about whether Luc would follow her or not, whether he would smile and go with her or not, whether he would hold out his hand and touch her or not... Oh, never mind, she thought angrily, shaking her head and raising her chin defiantly: if he did not follow her into the kitchen, she'd go up to her room and have a large cognac and read the book she had started...

But at that she crumpled. It seemed inconceivable suddenly: her loneliness crouched in her suddenly like a hungry lioness, ready to pounce on her books, her cognac, her letters home to people who found it impossible to understand her isolation, her self-willed exile, her internal alienation from all they offered her – her loneliness crouched, ready to consume those things and then look at her with prowling growls and circle her and force her out, out, into the world of real people...

And as if on cue, Luc came around the kitchen door. 'I'm going down to get the dessert. *Maman* has made a *tarte aux fruits* – Papa's favourite. We made a bit of money yesterday.' His eyes smiled with his mouth, teasing her, surely, she thought. 'Are you having dessert? They want me to get some Sauternes as well.'

What was he saying? That he knew she liked wine and he wanted her company?

'Oh, thanks, okay. I'll just finish this and wait for you.' She turned quickly away. Surely that was enough of a positive response to his encouragement, if that was what it was?

So they went in together. And she fiddled with her piece of tangy, berry-studded tart and its swirl of rich cream, and gulped her Sauternes, which was far too sweet for a palate craving courage. She listened distractedly to the conversation, trying not to look at Luc, but noticing an unusual confidence in his interaction with his stepfather, and catching his eye across the table and an oatmeal-coloured bowl of bramble roses anyway; and gradually she began to think, Yes, he will say yes. He is too inexperienced to make a move to me, but he wants me, he does want me; and her heart was full of hope.

*

Luc remained in the dining room with the men while Megan helped Mme Ravel and Mme LaGrange finish clearing up. The whole sexist arrangement would normally have had Megan fuming, but on this occasion she felt a strange sort of compassionate empathy with Luc. He was on the verge of entering a man's world; he had to learn their rituals and learn to be accepted by them as an equal. And he was in there, with the husbands, who might bed their wives in gratitude for care and selfless love…

Megan listened with only minor contributions to the women's gossip about the children and food. As usual now when they were together without the men, they cut her out of the conversation. Mme Ravel, under the influence of the more dominant woman, had started to treat Megan as Mme Lagrange did: as a servant.

But the work of clearing up and their steady chatter relieved her nervousness temporarily. How steady and uncomplicated their lives were, she mused. They had their own worlds, with children the stars of their orbits, and husbands minor moons. Cooking and clothes were their passions. Perhaps one day she would be the same, if she ever found someone who would love her enough to stay with her more than three months…but no, she corrected herself, no. She would never be like them. She was too ambitious, too educated, too little steeped in a culture. She would never feel she belonged to the world of the kitchen and nursery, the garden and sewing machine…

Perhaps, she recognised suddenly, sadly, she would never belong to the world of her own mother. Perhaps, if nothing else, these five months had taught her that much. She would always want something more, some excitement, some challenge, something outside the microcosm of the home. And the thought of sexual passion, sexual excitement, becoming dulled like a worn and blunted blade – oh, that was the most unacceptable of all!

She took her time clearing down benches and tidying things away. She volunteered to take the cold foods back down to the cellar. When she came up again, the women had returned to the dining room. She began to wipe a row of jars, mechanically, picking up each one and swiping the top, the bottom and around the convex glass, with growing nervousness. Would he never come in, bringing the last of the glasses or coffee cups, as he habitually did? And then she heard chairs scraping on the flagstones, and then the unmistakable timbre of his voice bidding everyone goodnight!

No, she thought, no! I've steeled myself for this; I can't just go to bed without speaking to him, without *finding out* how he feels about me! She thrust the jars hurriedly back against the wall and threw the dishcloth into the sink.

In the dining room, Luc was resting his forearms lightly on the back of a chair, nodding as his stepfather spoke to him. M. Ravel had gone and the two women were leaning towards each other under the candlelight, each with busy hands folding napkins, straightening the tablecloth.

'Well, I'm going to bed. Goodnight,' Megan said in French, moving gently toward the table.

They all raised their heads to her, each eye reflecting a candle flame.

'You're not going out for a walk tonight?' Mme Ravel asked in French.

'No. I'm tired.'

She nodded briefly, her plump hands resuming their folding. *'Eh bien: bonne nuit.'*

'Bonne nuit.'

'Bonne nuit.'

'Goodnight, Megan.'

She felt a flush of pleasure and renewed hope at Luc's English reply. She smiled at him, briefly but happily; then she dropped her gaze and moved out into the foyer and its dark staircase leading to her bedroom. She fumbled with the candles in the semi-darkness. Come on, she thought; come out to me!

And then he was there, coming out of the dining room in the yellow halo of a single taper taken from the table. 'Here,' he said, holding the candle out to her, 'take this one. I'll light another from it. There.'

Remarkably quickly, it seemed to Megan, he had her taper in a brass holder and one lit for himself; and he was turning toward the steps.

'Well, goodnight again.'

He turned to her to smile from the first step, and his eyes caught the light as he turned: and suddenly she was so frightened that he would actually go, leave her, give her no opportunity to speak to him, she said sharply,

'Wait! There's something I want to ask you. I need to talk to you – can you come up with me for a moment. It won't take long...'

'Up? To your room? Now?'

'Yes!'

He shrugged and she turned quickly and in her agitation half-tripped on a step; but recovered before he could put out a hand to help her. They walked side by side up the staircase, Megan trying to control her breathing, trying to get her heartbeat under control, Luc quietly, looking with a sideways frown at her, his footfalls light on the stone steps.

She fumbled with her door catch, then threw the door in too roughly and stumbled over to the bed. She placed her candle on the bedside table and turned to him abruptly.

He stood in the doorway, in the flickering light of his candle, looking at her, frowning.

She took a deep breath and said, 'Okay. I'll make this as quick as I can. Come in, please come in! I want to ask you something, but I don't really know whether you want me to or not. I don't want to embarrass you, or me, any more than I already have.' Her hands were shaking with the strength of her heart and her voice was thick and breathless. Slow down, she thought, slow down, you're rushing things, give him time…

But her courage was a hard lump of pain in her throat; although he had come into the room, he was staring at her with defensive, alien eyes.

He said, 'I'm sorry, I don't understand about what you speak. If you want to ask me something, then I think you should. Go ahead.'

'Well,' she breathed deeply and continued, 'I've been getting these messages from you.'

'Messages? I'm sorry, I haven't sent messages – you're mistaken.'

'Look. I think you know what I want to ask you. Do you want me to ask you or not?'

They stared at each other across the shadowy room, she defiant suddenly, he defensive.

'I don't have any idea what you want to ask me, no idea. So please, go ahead.'

'All right. Do you – oh God –' She dropped her face into her hands, feeling her cheeks burning, her hands damp. 'How do I say this?' She was almost laughing and he half-smiled uncertainly back. Then she lifted her head and looked at him fully. 'Do you – do you want to go to bed with me?'

He stared at her, his face frozen. There was a slight, laden pause, and then he said, 'What do you mean?'

Megan stared back at him, amazed. Slowly, deliberately, she repeated the question, this time in French, *'Tu veux coucher avec moi?'*

Then he reacted. *'Non!* No! I'm sorry if you thought I was sending you messages. I didn't mean, really –' His eyes were wild: he looked, Megan saw then, like a trapped animal.

'So you don't want to go to bed with me?'

'No, no, you're mistaken.'

'Okay. Well, just forget I mentioned it, okay? You'd better go.'

She lowered her gaze from his face to his hands, which held the candle at waist height, and she turned partly away, dazed, shocked: it seemed impossible that he had refused her and yet he had. She had so prepared herself mentally for his acceptance that all she could do was stand staring sideways at his hands, at their white, bony knuckles, and fight back an overpowering desire to reach out her own hands to touch him. Which she could not do.

He turned, quickly, with relief, she realised, and the light in the room faded gently, until its source was from only the candle she had placed on one of her books, next to her pad of writing paper, beside her empty cognac glass.

9

Boxing Day

'*Allô, oui?*' The voice is deep, clipped, unrecognisable.

'*Allô, Monsieur. Voici chez Dubois?*'

'*Oui, c'est ça.*'

'*Je m'appelle* Megan Falconer. *Je m'excuse de vous déranger à Noel, mais je voudrais parler à Luc Dubois, s'il vous plaît. Il m'attend.*'

Megan is conscious of the elaboration of her request, of its too-formal tone, but her hand has begun to tremble against the receiver. How ridiculous, she thinks irritably, that Luc should make her nervous after all these years – ten years! Especially since his letter was so friendly, so willing to please – not a hint of coldness or even awkwardness evident. She takes a breath and leans her back firmly along the glass of the telephone booth, pressing the fingertips of her gloved left hand against its iciness. The voice which answered – surely belonging to Luc's father? – has become a muffled drone and she can hear a faint background tinkle of piano music and conversation. Then there is a clatter as the receiver is lifted.

'*Allô*, Megan?' The voice is low, *intimate*.

She catches her breath. 'Luc.' Ridiculous, ridiculous, she thinks, that her heart should pound.

'Where are you?'

He is speaking English to her. She is instantly aware of it, and aware of her superstitious relief that he is. Because at the castle all that time ago, after she had so stupidly tried to seduce him, he had stopped speaking English with her and used only abrupt French. Her misery at that, more than at any of his other reactions, had been the most intense.

'I'm at a campsite at Checy. Odette – I told you about her in the letter – and I have a camping van.' A red light on the telephone begins to flash; she presses more coins into a slot with clumsy fingers.

'A camping van? In this weather?'

She almost laughs at the shock in his voice. 'Well, we didn't have much choice. Things haven't quite worked out to plan, and our budget is limited. Your country, you know, is expensive.'

'Yes, yes, I know but – in the snow?'

Quite suddenly she remembers him, at the castle, the first day she met him, bending to take the bag from her hand, his voice curiously tender and chivalrous in its American-tinged English, his blond hair falling across his face. Of course he must no longer look like that, any more than she looks the same as she did at twenty, although in all likelihood it is to that version of her he speaks…

'Yes, well, it's not the most pleasant of times to be doing this. But look, is it still possible to see you, to make a time to go to the castles? You said in your letter that –'

'Of course, of course, I have been expecting you. You must come here – have a meal with me and we can make our arrangements. It is better here than a restaurant – there is a baby, is there not?' His voice is hurried suddenly, nervous-sounding.

'Yes, Odette's baby. You're very kind, but – are you sure? It's your father and stepmother's house, isn't it? I don't want to intrude, especially at Christmas…'

The red light has started to flash again.

'No, no, it's fine, it's okay. They are going out tomorrow, but the maid will be here. You must come for lunch. You have the address? Just south of Orléans?'

'Oh, yes, and a map. Oh, look, my coins are about to run out –'

'See you tomorrow then – at midday?'

'Okay. And – thank you.' But her last word drops unheard along a deadened wire.

She holds the receiver uncertainly for a moment, then places it back in its cradle. When she steps out of the booth, she sees that the sky has darkened and the first stars have emerged from behind frost-clung clouds; faintly from the village, bells begin to chime.

*

In the weak winter sun, the wall surrounding the house and the house itself seem made of blocks of pale honeycomb, Odette thinks as Megan pulls the van off the wet bitumen onto puddled gravel. Snow is dredged in patches on a strip of deadened front lawn and on the bread-loaf curves of the wall; the stark branches of two ancient oaks cast a filigree of shadows over the house; the skeletons of two vines trace their black bones from barren front gardens up over deep windows and a recessed door.

Jason is asleep. Odette slips his sling from her shoulders carefully, unbuckles her seat belt, puts the sling back on and gathers Jason's nappy-bag. Then she turns to Megan, who has disappeared back into the cabin, and notes with surprise that Megan is *fussing* – she's changed her boots and is tidying her hair, peering into the van's tiny mirror. There's a streak of anxiety etched on her cheek.

'I'll lock up the front, shall I?'

Megan looks up at Odette swiftly. 'Uh, yeah, sure. I won't be a moment. There's a bottle of wine there, under the seat, I bought duty free – that's the one. Okay, I just need to put on some lipstick – God, my hair's awful. It's washing it in that tiny tub – never rinses properly. Oh, God, what the hell. What the hell am I worrying about? Shit. Come on. I'll lock the back. Got everything?'

'I think so. No, wait. Could you bring a tin of baby food? It's just – I don't want to wake him, and if I move too much –'

'Sure. This one do? Okay? Okay. Okay. Let's go.'

Odette hides a smile. Megan, Warrior Woman, she thinks, has a vulnerable heart. This Luc will be interesting. She hears the cabin door slam. And then she thinks, oh, God, I hope it works out for her. If not… She sighs, and steps down carefully into the crisp, cold air.

Megan takes the wine bottle from her and leads the way to the recessed, green enamelled door. There is a tarnished brass knocker, which she lifts and taps twice.

And then, to Odette, it seems as if they have stepped back to a time she has ever only seen in motion pictures.

A short, heavy-featured woman with the brown skin of the Portuguese opens the door to them. *'Entrez,'* she says thickly. She stands beside the door and indicates with her head where they should go: down a corridor, past an ornate hallstand on which heavy coats hang, to a dark oak interior.

There is a scent of garlic and frying onions leaking from somewhere in the house into drafts of the cold air flowing in from the open door, as well as the smell of polish and detergent. They walk down a strip of carpet toward shadows and increasing warmth. They pass two closed, varnished doors and then Megan goes to enter an open one: she sees a long table set with silver, light from deep windows in patches on the whiteness of the cloth.

But the woman, following them, says, *'Non – Monsieur est là-bas.'* She ushers them on and pushes them, almost, into the last doorway.

In an oak-panelled, ornately plastered room, Luc is standing beside the fire. He is wearing jeans and a dark wool jacket which reaches to his thighs; his head is bowed to the fire, his hands are in his pockets. She notices immediately that he has put on weight, that his body is fuller and heavier than she remembers it. And then she notices that his hair, the hair she remembers so vividly, is cut quite short and has darkened to the colour of damp straw, and is brushed back spikily from his temples so his face looks almost startlingly exposed.

When he looks up, his eyes are filled, Megan sees, with uncertainty…but he focuses on gentle, lovely Odette, with her night-black hair and curved Madonna arms and heavy Doc Martens: and his face clears. And then he faces Megan.

What does he think of me? she wonders. He's smiling and looks… what? Relieved? Why? Because I haven't changed much? I've cut my hair a bit, but it's still bobbed and I'm still thin enough and my face is much the same: more make-up on it perhaps – more sophisticated, hopefully; and I'm still wearing jeans, and I've put on that same colourful sweater, the one he liked, it seems not nearly ten years ago, which he perhaps will recognise although I have this awful anorak over it... Oh, but his eyes are the same, exactly the same as I remember them – long and slanted and blue as glimpses of summer sky, and I remember his nose with that hook to it; his skin has cleared, cleared nicely and is as pale as I remember, but his face has filled out, he's bulked up, no taller, but tall enough.

And then she's saying, 'Hello, Luc,' and smiling, walking towards him, clutching the bottle of wine with one gloved hand and holding out the other, so he takes her hand as he would a man's: then, confused, a little clumsily, bends to her and touches her face with his lips, first one cheek and then the other. Megan feels the softness of freshly shaved skin on her skin, and the heat of her rising blush.

'It is lovely to see you again,' he murmurs, straightening, her hand still held in his.

But, nervously, Megan immediately releases his clasp and transfers the wine to him instead. 'I brought you something, to say thank you in advance. It's really very kind of you to take us on – I really didn't mean for this job to land in your lap – it sort of got out of my hands.'

He turns the bottle and looks at the label automatically, then glances up sharply. 'But I am happy to help you – really. It will be a pleasure. But there was no need – such good wine.'

Their eyes meet briefly, gravely.

Megan turns quickly then, beginning to pull her gloves from her fingers and shove the soft leather into the pocket of her anorak – then thinks, oh, God, I should have waited. He was beginning to smile at me; why have I reverted to acting like an adolescent? – so says abruptly, 'Luc, this is Odette, and Jason, her son.'

Odette advances shyly, smiling, one arm around the slung sleeping baby, the other extended. 'Hello, how do you do? I'm pleased to meet you.'

Luc places the wine on the mantelpiece above the fire and takes her proffered hand, and when Megan looks up at him he is smiling warmly, his eyes turning up at the corners. Because Odette is so lovely, Megan thinks, or because it was the smile intended for me? It doesn't really matter surely, though? And then she thinks, well, perhaps it does – otherwise why would I be so nervous?

'How do you do. Odette – that's a French name, did you know? But of course you would know the ballet – *Swan Lake*, is it translated? You like the ballet? *Formidable! Eh bien,* would you like to put your baby – Jason? – down? He is heavy? The bedrooms are all heated.'

'Thank you. Oh, it's so wonderful to be in this warmth! You've no idea what it's like in the van. Although now that it's stopped snowing and the sun is out, it's not so bad.'

Luc is smiling at her still; an assured, relaxed smile. She makes him comfortable, Megan thinks, with a stab of jealousy: he can fulfill a male role, that of caring for a grateful female. Then, carefully, she thinks, no, it might just be that Odette is a welcome distraction from our awkwardness, the pressure of our past.

'This house,' Odette is saying, following Luc out of the room, 'is just beautiful. Just as I imagined a French country house to be. All these wooden beams and the thickness of the stone…' Her voice fades as their footfalls recede.

Megan breathes a sigh of suspended anxiety and turns to the fire. The flames leap at the air and crackle like rain on a tin roof.

She looks around the room fully for the first time. There is a tall, brightly decorated Christmas tree that had completely escaped her notice in a corner of the room, beside a dark-stained piano. Around the fire, three armchairs are arranged, and to the left of the fireplace is a deep window giving out onto a paved patio. The glass in the ten-paned frame is thick and greenish; one pane has a swirl, like the top of a whirlpool, in it. Megan looks absently through the glass as she holds her hands to the fire, and absently, she is struck by the beauty of the courtyard garden beyond.

A tree holds its black branches against the damp-darkened biscuit of the courtyard wall; in stark contrast, the morning's snow is settled like linen around the roots of the tree; a terracotta tub of dark green leaves stands poised on earthen tiles in a pale patch of sunlight. It is the light, she thinks, which is so moving: the colour of the light. The colour of the world under this light. It is something she has forgotten to notice.

'He sleeps so erratically,' Odette's voice is saying, coming around the doorway. 'Do you have any children?'

Megan is startled: it is something that hasn't occurred to her, that he might have been married once, or have children. But of course the Ravels would have told her – Mme Ravel has sent a Christmas card religiously every year, outlining important news about all the families Megan met, and about some she didn't – and after all he is only twenty-eight.

'No, no,' Luc is saying, 'no children. I am not married. But I have younger half-brothers and a half-sister – I learned about babies from helping with them. *Eh bien* – sit down, please! Yes there, by the fire, you need to warm – yes, good. Now, let me take your coats, and then something to drink – what would you like? Porto? Campari?'

Odette, sinking into a couch near the fire, hesitates, and looks at Megan, who is shrugging off her anorak; Luc turns to her too.

'Campari would be great, thanks,' Megan says, folding the coat over her forearm. 'I haven't tasted it in years. It's so very expensive in Australia. You should try it, Odette. It's very dry, and sort of bitter – unique. And warming.'

They both look at Odette, who is unclipping her coat.

She smiles and nods. 'Okay, thank you.'

'Megan, please – sit down. Let me take that. There – I'll put them in the hallway.'

Megan watches Luc in her peripheral vision when he comes back and begins to mix drinks at a sideboard. He is confident, she thinks: in that, he has changed. He is used to taking women's coats, and serving women drinks.

How are your family?' she asks from an armchair. 'The children must be practically grown up by now.'

'Oh, well, Eugenie and Pierre-Michel are both at *lycée* – high school? – and Paul is studying in Canada. They have all gone there to visit him for Christmas. The Ravels have gone with them: I expect you know that?' He hands her a glass. 'I had already planned to pass Christmas with my father and his wife, and I have been to Canada before.'

'Oh?' Megan is surprised: he had not seemed the travelling type ten years ago.

'Yes. I have been skiing there, with friends.'

'But you haven't been to Australia?' Odette takes the glass he proffers.

'Oh, no.' He looks surprised.

'Why would you want to?' she interjects quickly. 'It's so dry and modern, compared to this. I love the houses around here. They all seem made of the same stone. What is it?'

'It's called *tufa*: it's a soft limestone coming from this area.' He settles himself in the remaining armchair and leans forward; both the women see interest sparkle in his eye. 'When it is seasoned properly, it needs no other treatment to protect it. Most of the regions of France have a particular style because the houses are made from local materials... But this is what you would want to know for your article, Megan, I suppose?'

He looks at her quizzically, and she can't help noticing how the short hair and the extra weight on his face give him a softness, an approachability, without losing any of the youthful enthusiasm she was struck by ten years before.

'Yes – although more specifically to do with castles than architecture in general. Australians are pretty fascinated by castles, probably because we don't have any.' Megan sips her drink and smiles at him. 'I must admit, I was quite excited about staying in your castle years ago.' She watches him shrewdly, looking for any sign of embarrassment, but his face in the warm light of the dark-panelled and firelit room becomes thoughtful and serious.

'And this is why you have come back to France? For just this article? Surely not for a holiday as well, in winter?'

Megan glances at Odette. 'There is another reason, a more important one, but I'm afraid we can't tell you at this stage. It's to do with work. I hope you don't mind?'

'No, of course not. Although that does sound intriguing.' He smiles suddenly, the full, happy smile which she recognises, despite the extra weight, as ten years ago being her downfall – and because of it or in spite of it, she is moved again.

'The castle article is still important, though,' she says levelly. 'And your knowledge will be invaluable. And the fact that you can introduce us to people – get us access to photographs.' She is aware of sudden formality in her tone and in her expression, and for its reason: she thinks, this time, he won't see how he affects me quite so easily – this time, I will have a little sense!

But he is still smiling. 'To tell the truth, I like the…escape? Do you call it that? My father and his wife like me to visit with them, but it becomes a bit boring after a while – you understand? I pretend sometimes I have work to do to prepare for next year.'

Megan sees that he has developed a slight dimple in one cheek.

'Where do you work?' Odette has relaxed, curled in her chair, her long hair draped on the brocade, her Doc Martens hanging heavily over the edge of the seat cushion.

'I am a teacher. Of music and history. That should not surprise you, Megan.'

Again he smiles fully at her, the dimple deepening, and this time she is obliged to smile back. 'No. No, I guess not. Any more than it should surprise you that I am a journalist.'

'No…no, I am not surprised at that in the least.'

There is a pause: they are staring at each other and Odette sees that each smile becomes less certain.

'Well,' says Luc, and suddenly, abruptly, drains his glass: 'I think lunch should be ready. One good thing about staying with my father is that he loves good food and has an excellent cook. Come, please.'

*

It is after the soup and meat dishes that they hear Jason's cry.

'I'll need to breastfeed him.' Odette pushes back her chair with a sigh. 'I'll be a while – at least twenty minutes. Don't wait for me, please.'

Luc and Megan are silent for a moment after Odette leaves.

Luc picks up the bottle Megan has brought and refills their glasses. 'She is nice, your friend,' he says, a little awkwardly. 'How is it that you know her? She seems – younger – her clothes...' He tails off, aware of his clumsiness.

Megan smiles. 'Yes. She is. Twenty-one. It's okay, I know I look my age – I try to. Gives me authority in my job. And you're right, she's not really a friend – or at least wasn't before this trip... I met her through work, in a town called Rockhampton, in Queensland, the state – region – I live in.'

She pauses, but Luc doesn't fill the silence, only looks at her with his head slightly tilted; so she goes on, 'I was investigating a story there about black deaths in custody – that is, suicides of Aboriginal men in a prison – and I stumbled over another story. She was involved in it.'

'But how? She doesn't seem the type to have to do with prisons?' He stumbles a little over the phrase, but his face shows genuine puzzlement.

'Well, she isn't. She was a student...' Megan picks up her glass and handles it uneasily. She hasn't meant to say so much: the wine has made her careless. She should say nothing more: and it's not only journalistic caution but also a sense that she would be betraying Odette which makes her hesitate. Because if she told him the full story – of how Dickson, always in his police uniform, stalked Odette, then broke into her house, then blackmailed her into sexual favours, as the paper would put it, by threatening to hang heroin on Matt, how would he react? She knew so little of this older Luc – who could say how he, another man after all, might interpret the story?

It was not only Odette who knew that men could see such things entirely differently from women. Look at how Shakespeare, one of the most respected of men, portrayed Macbeth. His fall from grace all the fault of Lady Macbeth. Look at Genesis, for heaven's sake.

Of course, she could go into the detail she finally managed to get from Odette when she'd gained her trust – surely that would be enough to incense anyone? And tell him how Dickson hadn't been satisfied with fucking Odette just once, but had tried it again when Odette returned to Rockhampton in February, after the Christmas holidays – and how Odette, shaking, four months pregnant, had whispered the lie that it was over between Matt and her – and whispered that she wouldn't let Dickson do anything more to her. Ever. How Dickson had smirked and stared at her and she'd remained absolutely still until he'd shrugged and left; and four months later, just before the June holidays, Matt had been arrested for possessing half a kilogram of heroin.

Luc has been watching Megan's face all the while she has been think-ing. Now their eyes meet again, and Megan colours: Luc's gaze is in-tense. No, she thinks: I can't tell him any of that. It has nothing to do with him. It's Odette's story – or is at least until it hits the papers.

She shakes her head. 'I'm sorry – I can't tell you much more. Only that we're on the trail of a policeman who got away with planting drugs on Odette's boyfriend and landing him in prison. Odette managed to get the case delayed for five months because she made certain claims – but in the end she couldn't *prove* anything... Oh, but please don't see that as in any way saying Odette is involved in drugs. She isn't. She's... a victim in all this. That's all I can say.'

Luc picks up his glass and sips from it, leaning his elbows on the table. 'I think I have understood. So her boyfriend is in prison, now? And this is why you have come to France? But what can it have to do with France?'

'This policeman has a Spanish father. We're on our way to Alicante. Things were getting a bit...hot for him after I managed to get a fairly provocative report published in my paper – not naming names, of course. Our police department protects its own, you know, but only to a certain extent.'

Megan pauses again, biting her lip. Again she is aware of saying too much, and too quickly. 'Suffice it to say he decided that he might be safer in Spain,' she says more slowly and deliberately.

Luc is still frowning. 'I understand. You are tracking him – to interview him?'

'Yes.'

'But surely he won't…'

'Cooperate? No. But we have an idea about how to get him to talk, anyway. It's a long shot – which is why I have to do an alternative article, in case we fail – but we just might be able to pull it off. And if we do, Matt, Odette's boyfriend – Jason's father – will probably be released.'

Megan puts down her glass and leans forward, her shoulders hunching a little and her elbows on the tablecloth. Luc is silent for a moment – Megan can see him thinking. Then he glances up, sees that both their glasses are empty and automatically reaches for the wine bottle. There is a little left in it, which he pours carefully, so none of the lees escape.

'Well,' he says, 'I wish you luck. You and Odette. *Salut.*'

'Thanks. We'll need it.' She raises her glass to him as well, and drinks.

He pushes his chair back. 'Babetta has left: would you like some salad now? Or do you want to wait for Odette?'

'Oh, I'm sure she won't mind if we go on without her. She may be a while yet.'

Luc nods, and gets up.

You've got to hand it to the French, Megan thinks with a half-smile, leaning back and watching him leave the room: they don't let anything interfere with the progress of a meal. And they are very polite – hide their curiosity well. She herself would be itching to know the full story! But then, she muses suddenly, perhaps that is why I like him: because he is so different from me.

And abruptly she thinks, when he comes back, I'll talk about us. Quickly, today, before Odette comes back, or we'll go on being careful with each other and we might never bring it out into the open. And it's important to bring it out into the open, because I do like him, really like him a lot – he's so formal and well-mannered and…gentle…kind, or something. I've always liked him…that holiday in the castle – that was the pity of it. And I do want to find out – through curiosity, I suppose – why he rejected me. Because he did encourage me, surely – it couldn't all have been my imagination. Could he really not have been attracted to me at all? Or was it because of his religion? Or because he was too young, because I shocked him, because he was afraid?

But her heart gives a thrum, and she immediately thinks, no, I can't. I can't wreck this fragile friendship we've established again, and it doesn't really matter. It doesn't matter at all. I'll let it be.

She looks up with her heart still vibrating against her chest as Luc comes around the door, and he smiles faintly back. She buries her nose in her glass, quickly. He places a smooth wooden salad bowl on the table and takes another bottle of wine and clean glasses from the side-board; he opens the bottle expertly. He offers the salad to Megan, helps himself, pours fresh wine.

There is a silence.

Then Luc places his fork on his plate, the salad untasted.

Megan, her own fork halfway to her lips, pauses.

'I…' he begins. He leans back in his chair and flattens his hair back from his forehead with his hand; he looks at her speculatively. And she sees that there is a fine film of moisture on his upper lip.

'Megan – about the time when you…I wish to apologise.'

'Oh, but it's me who should apologise, I.'

'I thought about you a lot, you know.' His voice is suddenly soft: his eyes are full, gentle, like a child's with their fringe of lashes; he lowers his hand to the table.

'Did you?' Her voice is husky; she gulps some wine. 'I tried not to think about you at all. After I got back to Paris.'

'Our backgrounds were very different.'

She is silent. She thinks, go on. But he says nothing. Go on, she prompts silently – is that it? Is that the only reason you are going to give me?

'You haven't married?' His voice is still soft.

'No. I – travel too much. Put my job before my relationships, and not too many men like that. You must have thought I was terrible.'

'Terrible? I – didn't know what to think.'

She can't look at him. She stares at the ruby lights in the wine, willing him to go on, even though she knows that it shouldn't matter. Should it? It's not as if she still wants him, does she? It has to do with her ego, she decides abruptly: she wants him to say that he was attracted to her, that she had not read him wrongly, that under different circumstances, in a different place and time… But is it just that? Perhaps, more than anything, she wants to understand him.

She looks up. 'It was very foolish of me,' she says abruptly and quietly. 'Of course I realised that later. You've got to understand, though, how lonely I was. I'd been stuck with the Ravels for five months, my mother was dead, I couldn't even write to her, my father had married again, instant new family – and there had been this boy in Australia… I thought he loved me, but he didn't. It all made me…a bit reckless.'

He puts his hand out and gently covers her hand, the one fiddling with the base of her wineglass. 'You were not terrible. Only – different. And I wish I had not acted so – badly. I did not know what to do. Nothing like it had ever happened to me before. Or again. While I was waiting for you to come this morning, I thought that this is what I most want to say to you.'

Megan smiles then, but uncertainly; she drops her head, then lifts it and turns her palm up to clasp his. 'Well,' she says, 'I can't say the same.'

10

Wintered Dreams

When Odette returns with Jason clinging like a possum to her side, she finds them huddled over a map, open hardcovered books scattering the table. A new bottle of wine has been opened and a lavish platter of cheeses and red and gold fruit glimmers like a dish of uncut jewels in the light and against the white cloth. They both only notice that she is back when she speaks.

'Is it okay if I heat this baby food? No, don't get up. I'll find my way to the kitchen. Does your cook speak English? Although I'm sure I can make her understand.'

'No, no.' Luc has pushed back his chair. 'Sit down, please. Let me take that. Babetta has gone. There is a microwave oven – here, it will only take a minute. Really, it is easier this way. I won't be long.'

Odette sits down tentatively at the table, juggles Jason, and glances at Megan, who has watched Odette's interchange with Luc absently; then Megan shakes herself, as if she has been in a dream, and briskly sits up.

'Well, 'Dette,' she says, picking up the wine bottle and offering it, 'prepare for more snow. The Massif Central has had heavy falls, but Luc thinks we should be able to get to three or four castles near his without too much trouble, so that's where we're heading tomorrow. He says he can ring the caretaker of his castle, who'll clear the tracks for us. I'll need to take photos and get a rundown on the history and architecture of each place. But there is a bright side: we'll be able to stay in Luc's castle, overnight or perhaps over two. And with its fireplaces, believe me, we should be warm. We'll take the van up: he offered to drive us, but I think it's easier if we just take the van and we can carry on to Spain as soon as I have enough material. Okay with you?'

Odette sips the wine and carefully places it away from Jason's exploring fingers. She gives him a teaspoon, cupped end down, which he immediately puts in his mouth. She strokes his downy head. 'But I thought we would be heading straight down to Alicante tomorrow? I mean, this has been two days already, and you said...'

'Yes, I know. But Luc has the time off now – he has to go back to work in a week – it's the ideal opportunity to get this article. Dickson won't go anywhere, you said that yourself. I'll ring Pete's contact tonight, see if he's traced Dickson. But even if he has, we still don't need to rush down there. I'm sorry: it does mean being in the van longer – but as I said, we'll be able to stay in the castle, sleep in beds, have hot baths. Then we'll shoot down to Spain, get the interview, and you can fly out from Alicante. What's today? Monday? You'll be on a plane back to Australia by Sunday, guarantee it.' Megan curls a strand of hair behind her ear; there is just a trace of anxiety in the gesture.

'Well... I guess you're right. I suppose it was me who asked you to stop in the first place.' Odette is frowning. 'You have to do the article – I realise that. I guess it's not going to make any difference if we're delayed a few more days.'

Jason has been looking up at her as she speaks: now he reaches for a tear-shaped pendant she has on a leather thong around her neck, and clutches it. She disengages his fingers gently.

'And to tell you the truth, I'm not looking forward to seeing him again, going through with this. I suppose I just want to get it over with, want it to be in the past.'

Megan watches Odette's skilful averting of Jason's attention from the pendant to a crust of bread, and feels sudden compassion for her. Odette asks so little, Megan thinks, but has such responsibility. And of course, she must be dreading like a demon facing Dickson.

'Sorry it's been so tough for you,' she says quietly. 'But it'll be worth it, you'll see. And you said you wanted to see a bit of France, that you might never come back.' She has suddenly remembered that.

Odette shrugs, and frowns again. 'Yes, that's true. And I'm trying not to think about what will happen in Spain until we get there, so at the moment it's mainly the cold that worries me…so I guess if we can stay warm, it'll be okay.'

She looks down at Jason, who chews the crust for a moment, staring at his mother with wide blue eyes, then he jiggles and crows, and suddenly smiles.

*

'Come, Odette, I think we must leave Megan to make some notes now. It is warmer in the lounge room for *le petit* also.'

They have finished coffee and Jason is wriggling and squirming in Odette's arms; Luc is collecting a pile of rejected books to the left of his coffee cup.

Megan hesitates, looking at him for a moment. From the time of his letter assuring her of his willingness to help with the article, she resolved to remain friendly to but aloof from him, to *this time* be in control, unaffected by him, to show him that this contact was purely coincidental and business-like. But now, now that he has teased her and flattered her, perhaps even flirted with her, she has a strong impulse to say, damn the notes: stay, talk to me. But her professionalism demands she take advantage of the books, from his own collection and also from the local library, so she says smoothly, 'Thank you, if that's okay? I'll only need about an hour. Maybe a little more. Then we'd better be getting back to the camping ground.'

'The camping ground? But it is so cold. You should…you must…'

'No.' Megan interrupts him. 'You don't need to offer to put us up, thanks all the same. We can make the van quite warm, it's okay. All our gear's in there as well, so it's much easier to just stay put. Really.'

Luc hesitates, but Megan senses his relief at her insistence. It is after all not his home, and the older French, she seems to remember, do not take strangers under their roofs too easily.

She resolves to tell Odette that, later.

Which she does, over reheated leftovers of their Christmas feast and the remains of a bottle of wine; and Odette nods in acceptance, noticing that Megan has the gas heater going. She asks about Luc, and Megan tells her in a little more detail about her month in the castle as an au pair with the Ravels and Lagranges, and adds that in those days Luc wrote music and poetry, and wanted to get back to nature. Odette watches her face, noting Megan's sudden preoccupied silences, and then glimpses of suppressed excitement, as she relates her story; and Odette thinks, there was something between them. Probably still is. Then Megan gets up suddenly, exclaiming, saying she's almost forgotten to ring Pete's contact in Alicante; and Odette presses nothing further.

*

Megan, to her guilty relief, discovers little about Dickson: he has still not been traced, but is assumed to be in Alicante. Odette nods drowsily from her sleeping bag when Megan returns, but Megan herself settles to restless sleep, despite the day's wine – then in the morning wakes brisk with an anticipation she swiftly curbs. But she sweeps a heavy-lidded, thrice-woken Odette up in her energy, so that by the time Luc arrives at ten in his smart, cherry-red Renault, they are ready to follow him.

*

Quite soon after they begin the journey, Odette's head droops and she dozes; and Megan, her initial excitement about the trip settling, reluctantly steers her mind to more logical and habitual analysis. All right, she thinks, what of it? What of the fact that Luc's flirting with me, and he's coming with us to the castle? That Luc knows as well as I do that if he wrote a letter of introduction I would probably fare just as well in getting material; and he could have trusted me with the keys to his mother's castle so that Odette and I could have stayed there anyway.

Okay, all right, when that flash of inspiration came to do this back-up article, I did entertain the idea of seeing him again – he did send me that poem, after all – but I didn't expect anything like *this* contact with him. But here it is: handed to me on a platter. Here he is, handed to me on a platter, perhaps?... Oh, God, she thinks, oh, God: here I go again...

Wanting him. Wanting Luc. Why? Because I'm attracted to him, yes. But I've been attracted to lots of men, and haven't been this obsessive about them. Because he's French, he's connected obscurely with my mother? Possibly. I acknowledge that I've always been a bit loopy about France, the French way of life. Or is it only because I want to...finish something? What? Something that needs finishing? Or do I mean *beginning*?

She sighs. It shouldn't be important. He is just a boy who has become a man, who annoyed her, irritated her, then somehow wooed her into liking him. Not only through his face, the grace of his body, his physical appeal, she realises suddenly, but also through his talk, his overt searching for a way to live his life, his desire for a simplicity of living juxtaposed with his desire through his poetry to be a spokesperson for his age, a desire which in a curious way mirrored her own...

Yes, that is what fascinated her about him. What still fascinates her.

*

They stop only once, outside Moulins, to feed Jason, and for fuel and a lunch of salami, tomatoes and bread and cheese, eaten on the snow-slippery tarmac of an extensive petrol depot while they stamp their feet and breathe great clouds of vapour with sips of coffee.

After that, it begins to snow and Megan is hardly aware of the route they take, concentrating instead on the red car ahead and the slippery, snow-banked road. She notices that they are climbing, and that the snowdrifts are deepening, and that they pass several major towns: only when they turn off the main highway does she begin to look with interest again at road signs. And recognises none of them.

And so is surprised when the Renault pulls smoothly onto a snow-clogged, but recently cleared, track and begins a suddenly familiar ascent: her heart gives a quick, unexpected leap as she glimpses a sharp white turret through snow-drenched branches. But of course it is all so different from when she last saw it: gone are the thick green foliage and rambling roses and lush undergrowth, and in their place are sharp, snow-stiff twigs fingering a pale sky, and white fields and a white valley broken only by stony farmhouses and shelters. She looks eagerly to where the chickens had been, but the snowy yard is deserted and sterile-looking; there is no goat, and the vineyard is only blackened, snow-furred knots, as neat and forbidding as barbed wire.

Luc opens the gate with difficulty, and she lumbers the van in after the Renault and pulls it to a stop beside his car. As the engine splutters out, she turns to Odette, who's waking, stretching her back and opening reluctant eyes, and sees through her window Luc, bulky in a heavy greatcoat and woollen cap, heading back to close the gate.

'We're here,' she says, unnecessarily.

Odette blinks and looks up at the castle. It is pale grey in the fading light, its turrets pointed and sharp and stiffly white. It looms above her: three storeys high with the round turrets adding four higher other rooms in its corners. Tall, narrow windows are set symmetrically in its walls, their deep sills pillowed with snow, their glass shiny as icy eyes. A wet brown fuzz of dead vine sits like a straggly beard around the downturned mouth of an arched doorway.

'What do you think?'

'It looks…daunting. Forbidding.'

Wind suddenly flops against the van and the dead vine ruffles and stirs as if in anger; Odette shivers instinctively, but Megan is staring, her eyes bright, up at the turrets.

*

Luc places down his burden of gas bottles and unlocks the arched door, which is in fact two doors, like shutters; then he unlocks internal French windows. '*Entrez!*' he says, smiling, standing back.

Odette, in the lead with an awakening Jason, hesitates, then steps in first. The interior is dark, and for a moment all Odette is aware of is a dank, mossy smell; then her eyes adjust and she sees that she is in a broad stone corridor which seems to run like a tunnel through the centre of the castle. Ahead of her, the apparent meeting-point of perpendicular corridors, is a sweeping stone staircase; to the left and right of her are open doors, leading to presumably corner rooms of the castle.

'To the left!' Luc calls; and Odette finds herself in a large bare room with a stone-tiled floor and stained plaster walls, originally cream.

There is a blackened chimney place set in an internal wall, and all around the western window opposite it are large pale spots, as if round pictures, there for a long time, had quite recently been removed. There is a primitive-looking bench underneath the window, lit greyly by the magnifying effect of a slanted, metre-deep recess around the panes. The air is icy.

'My God, what's happened?'

Megan's voice behind Odette is sharp, and Odette turns to see Megan, hair flicking across her face in her agitation, swing to Luc.

Luc places the heavy gas bottles on the ground again and looks up at Megan apologetically. 'Well, we don't come here so much now. M. Pouget – he has a castle I will take you to tomorrow – wanted to buy some furniture from here, and so we sold him the best pieces, and the rest we have packed away in a locked room. He offered a good price. The furniture was – what is the word? – becoming marked, stained – and we thought it better to sell it. One day, if one of my family wants to fix things, we can buy new furniture. You're disappointed?'

'Well –' Megan has turned away from him back to the bare, cold room, and Odette sees she is frowning, the blonde edges of her hair framing her profile '– it's just…it seems so *neglected*. As if you've abandoned it. And I thought you were planning to live here, you, on your own, I remember you saying that… It had such a style before, such an other-worldly…'

'Megan?'

Both the women look back at him at his tone, and see his eyebrows raised in teasing amusement.

'Have you become a romantic now?'

'No! No – of course not! But the furniture was right here, it belonged here: now it seems so, I don't know…'

'But after all, in life what you wish to do, what you wish to have, is not always possible. My mother has debts, like other people. The price of this place – to keep it from thieves – it was best to sell the valuable things, to stop the stealing. Or to stop their ruin.' His voice is sober, but gentle. 'But there are some pieces we can bring in here to warm the room – some thick curtains and rugs and some couches… But first, it is important is to get the fire burning before it is dark. It is dark so soon in winter. I'll connect the *gaz*, and bring up some firewood. The fire will warm the hot water tank – you remember, Megan? The tank is in the wall behind the fire – in the kitchen, actually. Then you could make something hot to drink, perhaps? You remember how to work the cooker? Okay. That at least will have changed only a little, and some of the other rooms also.'

He smiles at her suddenly warmly, but Odette sees that Megan is still frowning.

*

But in terms of the kitchen, Megan thinks, as she fumbles with cold fingers to light the gas stove and the bits of candle Luc has produced, he is right. For the stone basins and broad wooden draining boards and rough-hewn benches are just as she remembers them, and the floor is as worn and smooth and unevenly patterned in its stones as she has seen it in her most recent dreams. In her most recent dreams…

She tips tinned soup absently into a pan, stirs it, then turns to the deep kitchen window and stares intently out into the thickening greyness. Across the valley she can make out white ridges of terracing, which in summer would be green with fruiting vines, and against the snow the dark geometric shapes of other dwellings: farmhouses, temples, barns. But there is nothing she can see there which is familiar: not a building she can recall in any detail, not a single tree she recognises.

But, she thinks, shuddering suddenly and turning away, back to the familiar stove, that's because it is winter. Everything looks so different in winter. Underneath, nothing has really changed.

*

Although it's only five o'clock, it is quite dark by the time Luc has a fire going and has rigged up curtains and rolled out rugs, Megan has fetched crockery and cutlery from the van, and Odette, wrapped in her sleeping bag and a deep sofa Luc has found, has breastfed Jason. The coldness of the castle room recedes gradually as the logs begin to take the flame, and, with relief because she has been nursing him for most of the day in his sling, Odette puts Jason on a rug in front of the fire. He has not yet begun to crawl, but lies on his back and stretches his hands to the dancing fire, cooing to it.

'Cognac, anyone?' It is Luc, still in his coat and cap, who offers it, bearing a dusty bottle and thick shot glasses on top of an extra basket of logs he has brought up from the cellar.

Megan, placing bowls and a pot of soup on a low table Luc has brought from somewhere else in the castle, pauses momentarily; and Luc, with a raised eyebrow and half-smile, meets her eye.

'You see, I remember,' he says, the smile deepening. Then he squats beside the fire and fills the glasses, saying, 'There, this is warmer already. I'll bring bedding down here tonight, to sleep. The big bedroom has a fire and furniture, so you will want to sleep there, I imagine.' But he is pouring cognac, and so addresses that to neither of them directly. '*Eh bien, voilà*. This will warm you.'

He waits until Megan has seated herself and taken her glass from him before raising his and saying, '*Salut!*' and catching her eye again.

Megan flashes a smile back. And Odette, watching them, raises her eyebrows and drinks too.

'Oh, that's good.' Megan places her glass down, then picks up the ladle. 'The soup's not much – tinned, I'm afraid. But anyway, it will get us through until we can cook something more decent.'

'To tell you the truth, I have had tinned soup before, you know.' Luc is refilling his glass; he lifts it and looks at the colour of the cognac in the firelight before adding, 'In fact, when I first moved into an apartment, away from my mother, I drank litres of it. And I was buying sauces in bottles. And frozen hamburger meat! And even frozen pizza! I'm ashamed to say it, but it is the truth.' Both Odette and Megan see his eyes twinkle in the firelight. 'You must not be in awe of my culture, Megan. We have the convenience as much as anyone else.'

'I –' Megan has coloured, although the other two see it only in the dim light as a slight heightening of the fire warmth which has already made her cheeks pink '– I...well, it's just that when you were younger your family insisted on everything being fresh: you know, you had chickens and the goat for milk and cheese and the orchard and the vineyard, and they baked bread...'

'Yes. But it has been ten years since then, Megan. And France has had a very big influence from America. She – it – America, I mean – is difficult to resist: we have MacDonald's now, a Disneyland near Paris.'

'I know, I know! I'm a journalist! But surely it hasn't touched the heart of your culture – your pride – your way of living? I mean, surely there are things you hold sacred? Things of quality which are yours, unique, which the rest of the world looks up to? Why do you think Australians want to read an article about French castles? Or French wine, or art, or sculpture or food?' Megan's voice is controlled, but has an edge of defence, which she recognises herself. 'Here,' she says more quietly, 'have the soup before it gets cold. Odette? And some bread? Luc?'

'Thanks. It smells great.' Odette dips her bread and has a spoonful of soup, then, sensing Megan's agitation, says quickly, turning to Luc, 'You've a long way to go before your culture's anywhere near as commercial as ours. Oh, except with one thing – we can't seem to get fresh milk here. That just seems really bizarre, out of place. There are aisles and aisles of all sorts of other fresh foods in the supermarket, and then aisles and aisles of long-life milk, but no fresh milk. How come?'

Luc stops eating, his hand suspended over his bowl, then says, 'Well, I'm not sure. Myself, I buy fresh milk easily, in Paris. Perhaps it is the convenience, again? Or perhaps it is that people don't trust fresh milk any more. Since Chernobyl, and other health scares.'

'Ah.'

Both Megan and Odette are silent for a moment. They all resume eating. The fire flames suddenly, sending sparks up the chimney, and Jason starts; Odette bends to reassure him.

To break the silence, which seems to her becoming awkwardly pro-longed, Megan says, 'The chimney seems to be clear. Does anyone look after the castle now? You used to have caretakers, didn't you?'

'Yes, we did. Now there is some one who comes by once a week in the winter, and sometimes people – tourists, the English – pay us rent to stay here in other seasons. We have enough furniture in storage for them. There is nothing otherwise to steal now, and it's away from the main roads. We have been lucky so far. We bring the *gaz* bottle with us, and the firewood and preserved foods are locked away. My mother still likes to harvest the cherries and *cassis* – blackcurrants? – and bottle them every year. She is not quite as corrupted as I am.'

Again, Odette sees his eye sparkle, but Megan has her head down, fumbling in a pocket of her anorak. 'Wait – wait a sec. I'll get some paper and get that down. You don't mind, do you? I'll do a proper interview, taped and everything, later or perhaps tomorrow, whichever suits you.'

Luc looks at her for a moment, considering. Then he turns to Odette. 'She was not like this, you know, when I met her ten years ago. Not so interested in this way of life.' He has an eyebrow raised inno-cently. 'She drank cognac then, it is true, but she laughed at me.' His voice is solemn. 'Nevertheless, there were the long brown legs and... other things...I felt I had to entertain her.'

Megan's head is up, her eyes round with indignation. 'Entertain...'

'Of course I was not the only one who noticed these things. Who could miss them? Even my stepfather, when we went to Montpelier…' But no, you don't want to hear that…' He turns at last to Megan, his dimple hovering and his eyes very blue and lucid in their innocent fringe of lashes.

Odette watches Megan's face relax and her lips curve slowly upward. How much prettier she is when she smiles, she thinks.

'Shouldn't we be getting organised before it gets late?' Megan has her head on one side, looking at him archly.

Luc places his bowl on the table and stands up, turning back to Odette with a sigh. 'This I remember too: she was always working.' He looks sideways at the intake of breath.

Megan slowly closes her mouth.

He shrugs then, and his voice becomes businesslike. 'But yes, she is right. I will need to start the other fire and make sure no pipes have frozen. You should bring in from your van what you need for the night and morning now, before the freeze sets in entirely. I have been here only twice before in the winter, but I do remember how cold it can become in the night.'

'Of course, yes. And Luc, don't worry about sheets for us – we'll bring in our sleeping bags and sleep in those: there's no point in having to wash sheets we've only used for a night.' Megan keeps her voice measured and calm.

Luc hesitates, then says, 'Yes, you're right. Although it may be two nights yet.' He bends to the fire to adjust a log, kneeling beside Jason who gurgles to him and to whom he clicks softly back; then he picks up the basket holding the rest of the wood. 'The bedroom is to the left of the first landing, up the stairs. You saw the stairs before?' He speaks only to Odette, who nods. 'The bathroom is beside it: the water is heated by the fire, and the pipes are quite new, but I will need to check them. Also to check there are no unwanted visitors up there!' He grins his sudden grin at Odette's startled face and Megan's up-jerked head, then he turns to the doorway with the basket and throws over his shoulder, 'But I'm sure our noise should have frightened them off by now.'

*

'What do you think he meant?' Odette, praying that she will have time to collect what she needs before his abandoned cries become too strident, has left Jason beside the fire, and is throwing toiletries and nappies and clothes into a plastic bag. 'About unwanted visitors, I mean.'

'Oh, I don't know.' Megan is rummaging in the van's cupboard for breakfast food. 'Maybe he's just teasing us. Why would anyone want to stay in a freezing castle with no means of heating anything? It didn't look as if anyone had been in the kitchen, or if they had they were pretty neat. Anyway, he's right. If anyone was here, they would have skedaddled when they heard us arrive.'

'Yes. And I feel safe with Luc anyway. He's nice, isn't he? Bit stunning too.' Odette picks up a bottle and studies the label before throwing it in the bag. 'Oh God, I've got to get back to Jason: he's not keen on separation. Not that I can blame him in this climate. What do you want me to take to eat? The fresh stuff?'

'It's okay. Leave that to me. Do you really think he's stunning?'

'Don't you?' Odette's eyes are round and innocent.

'Well...not stunning, but nice, yes. Trying hard. Quite nice-looking. He's fleshed out a lot. Not stunning, Odette: he's hardly that!'

Odette shrugs and picks up the bag. 'You sure you want to sleep with me? Jason's not the easiest person to spend the night beside. I'm sure you'd have a better night if you slept down near the main fire...'

'Odette!'

Odette swings around at the sharpness in Megan's tone.

'Look...I tried it on him, okay?' Megan lowers her voice, softening it. 'Before, when I was twenty. He wasn't interested. So no more of that, all right?'

They look at each other fully for a moment. Then Odette says quietly, 'I think he's interested now. I'll disappear quickly tonight. Give him a chance, okay? Provided he has got rid of any unwanted visitors, of course: otherwise you'll be rudely interrupted! She grins and swings out of the van before Megan can say anything more.

11

Castle Squatters

'So tell me, Odette, what do you think of my mother's castle?' In the bedroom, Luc leans back on his heels from stacking logs beside the flaring fire to turn to Odette, standing on a chair hooking up curtains.

Jason lies in a nest of blankets in the middle of the double bed, watching with fascination candle and firelight flicker on his mother and on the pale walls and dark brocade of the curtains. Megan, downstairs, has volunteered to make the rest of their evening meal.

'Well, I…' Odette hesitates, bringing her arms down from the curtain folds for a moment: 'It's so gothic, isn't it? Reminds me of vampires and witches – "The Lady of Shalott" even, locked in her tower of loneliness… Oh, you wouldn't know that – an English poem.'

'"The Lady of Shallot?"' Luc pronounces the last word with difficulty. 'But, yes, I think I know it.'

'Oh, sorry. Of course – I forgot. Megan said you write poetry, so I guess you'd read it too, wouldn't you? Even in English?' She slips two rings over the wooden rod.

'A little, yes. And I don't write so much any more. But don't tell Megan that.' He smiles, his eyes flashing in the firelight.

'Really?'

Luc shrugs. 'I have had some poems published. One, I sent to Megan: it always reminds me of her. She in a way helped me to write it well – not actually, but she put the idea of how to fix it there. Sorry, I'm speaking badly. Anyway, I've had other poems published, here and there – but only in small magazines. My mother in fact has something to do with it, some influence. Perhaps the poems are good but I'm not sure.' He shrugs again and goes back to arranging the logs. 'Lately, I can't seem to write much, in any case. There's my job, films to see, and I play in a band…all sorts of escapes.'

Odette catches the quick smile he throws over his shoulder, and feels unsettled by it; but she can't think of anything to say in response, so goes back to threading hoops.

*

Megan fries the Alaskan salmon Odette bought on Christmas Eve in butter and onions, then adds white wine from a *brique*, a tetra pack. She pours herself a glass of the wine as well and winces at its tartness, but drinks it anyway. The kitchen is warmed by the stove. She thinks of Luc's smile and his teasing, his deliberate, clear flirtation. She mixes a little oil and vinegar in a wooden bowl then rubs it with garlic and adds lettuce leaves, black Greek olives, slices of tomato, onion and capsicum. I'm trying to impress him, she thinks. Feed him: the way to a man's heart is through his stomach. Does she want his heart? Perhaps not, she thinks, draining her glass recklessly: perhaps only his body. Temporarily? Of course, the heart would be a good thing to have: with it would come that joy, that indescribable joy, that astonishment at waking up thrilling with the day ahead…not to mention the possibility of this castle, French citizenship, her mother's culture to call her own at last…

Then she sighs. I swore I would not do this, she thinks. I swore I would not allow myself to fantasise, to start dreaming about him and about wanting to live in France again, to be French…

But surely, one must have dreams? Castles in the air, castles in the sand, castles in Spain – or in France, in this case… Why castles? she thinks suddenly. Why do I think of dreams in terms of castles? Because castles are symbols of the possibility of romance, of the ethereal, of supernatural happiness…but also symbols of power and wealth, the twin gods of the Western world? And castles in the air or in the sand offer – what? An illusion, an unreal dream…but a blueprint for something one should try to make real, if only temporarily, if only symbolically, if only once?

She pours more wine into her glass. What do I really want? she thinks. I want to live in France. That's part of it. There's no point in denying it. It's a love affair with France that I want, surely? I want to escape the sun-glaring heat of Brisbane and the parochial infighting at the paper, the spongy white sandwiches and instant coffee and men who think weekends are about watching football or going surfing, and a meal out is at Sizzler or Pizza Hut, or else at a classy restaurant where they complain about the small helpings or the slowness of the service, and drink Scotch and Coke or beer all night and then grope you in the taxi. All right, the grass might look greener here – but it's pretty brown over there in that drought, and I'll take my chances, if the chances are offered.

But Luc, what of him? Am I really only interested in France? She sighs and looks up at her reflection in the warped window glass, and out into the darkness beyond. And thinks, oh, of course: of course I still want him. He has still those sea-coloured eyes… He's lost some of his idealism, I think, his passion for purity in living, but still there's his love of history, his wish for simplicity, his interest in music… What did I expect: that the attraction would have vanished with my youth? That because he's heavier and older I wouldn't feel drawn to him any more?

And here we are, astonishingly, in his castle again, by some twist of luck, or some whim of the gods, able to replay a comedy from ten years ago. But how will it end this time? Would real contact between us bind – or bruise? We are back to skating around each other, but this time we know what is underneath, both of us: we are adults now, wise and free of families and fear…

But if we do have sex, what then? Am I going to be able to cope with then leaving, going to Spain, not seeing him again?

Perhaps if I sleep with him here, tonight… And so she struggles with her own desire.

*

Odette watches the other two as they all eat, around the fire downstairs again. Jason, fed and bathed, is asleep on his rug near her feet, so she has the time and inclination to indulge in a type of voyeurism. The wine they are drinking and the thick, tender chunks of fragrant fish in her mouth combine with the warmth of the fire to give her a kind of sleepy sensual pleasure in the obvious sexual tension between Megan and Luc. Curiously, she realises that she feels no sexual longing for Matt, Jason's father, in response to her observation of their flirtation; only a sudden yearning for the warm, close comfort of Matt's body in a bed with hers. Or perhaps, she consoles herself quickly, only for a deep, warm bed itself.

'This fish is really excellent.'

'Oh, thanks.' Megan sips her wine and looks sideways at Luc. She's about to say, 'It's very easy to cook, though,' but pulls herself up. Instead she says almost softly, 'And the wine is beautiful.'

Odette looks at the flash of smiles between them as they lift forks and wineglasses, and realises that she is gradually becoming invisible to them. The wine has worked its magic, she thinks then, for the first time fully confident: Megan would not share her bed that night.

*

'I wonder –' Megan hesitates, wiping her hands on a damply cold dishtowel, then hanging it on its rack and straightening its folds.

All three have cleaned up the dishes, but Odette has quickly disappeared, 'To put Jason to bed'; Luc is tidying away the final plates in the fluttering candlelight.

'Yes?' Luc pauses and turns to her solemnly.

And Megan has a sudden strong urge to say, 'If you might fuck me now?' just as solemnly and blandly as he has questioned – but despite the amount of wine she has drunk, she doesn't. Instead she says, 'If we might go up to the turrets? I wanted to go up on my own, before dinner, but what you said about unwanted visitors threw me a bit... I wasn't sure what you meant. What did you, by the way?'

'Mean? Oh, you know – what are they called? Squatters – or there might have been rats, or ghosts even. It's always best to make sure.'

'Luc.'

'No – seriously. There have been rumours in the past, you know – noises in the night, stories of attacks on children.'

'By ghosts?' Megan's eyes are incredulous

'No – rats. Surely you, Megan, don't believe in ghosts?'

'You're teasing me.' She's smiling back at him.

'Yes.' They are suddenly speaking in French. 'You like it, don't you?'

Her eyes are soft and dark and her pale hair falls straight and silky around her face. 'The teasing? Yes.'

'Good. Then let's go. To the tower.'

'Shall we take some cognac?'

'Of course.'

'It's much better than mine was.'

'One improves with age. Or one's taste does.'

*

Odette's door is closed. Luc's feet scrape on the stone landing as he passes her room, but there is no other sound except their own faint, quick breathing; in the light of the candle, there is only their powdery breath moving and their shadows.

As they mount, the air becomes increasingly warmed: the heat from the two fires, Megan realises, is seeping up to the highest recesses of the castle.

Luc leads her to his turret, the one on the right. The door creaks as he pushes it open; Megan, behind him with the candle, sees his great-coated shadow hugely magnified in the round room. The bed is where she remembers it, jutting out from the curved turret wall beneath the lozenge-shaped window, still with a white counterpane, still with a round wooden table beside it and a sofa chair, recognisable under a dust cover, against a wall opposite. Only the desk is missing.

Luc places the cognac bottle and shot glasses on the table. He turns to her.

'It's not as cold as I imagined.' She's speaking in French.

'No.'

'But looks exactly the same.'

'It's been the same for many centuries.'

'How many?'

'It was built in the twelfth. You can tell from the architecture, and there are records in the village. I believe these turrets were used as look-out posts, but also as prisons. Occasionally, in times of peace.'

She can see his ironic smile even though he is half turned away to pour the cognac. 'Oh, but I meant the furniture – the way it's arranged – it looks the same as it did ten years ago. Remember, you played that song and I sat on that sofa, and the counterpane was the same, only there was a moon, moonlight?'

For now, there is only a black arched window, as impassive as a mirror, reflecting their flickering selves.

'I remember.'

'Do you? I thought you were going to make a move on me, asking me up to "look at your etchings".' Although they are still speaking in French, she says the phrase in English, very softly.

'I'm sorry?'

'Oh, don't worry: it's a…cliché. I thought you were –'

He's sitting on the bed, pouring cognac into the glasses. He says, 'Yes.'

Megan draws breath. She stares at him, feeling suddenly then a familiar rising irritation: and this time she can't help it. She says, 'Yes? What do you mean, yes? That you know the expression?' She's still standing, although he is sitting on the bed.

'I mean that I know – now – that you must have seen it that way.' He's looking at her, smiling gently. 'Come – here. You haven't lost the taste for cognac? I have only recently acquired it. We French are slow learners. Or slow acquirers, at least.' He hands her a glass then holds up his own in a salute before draining it.

Megan sits on the edge of the bed and sees then that he is slightly drunk: his eyes are as glassy as a still sea and his fringe has begun to spring spikily forward.

He says carefully, 'I didn't really want to – well, you know I was young for my age – immature – it was incredible to me that you might actually think…be prepared –'

'To go to bed with you?' *Me coucher avec toi?* She says it very softly in its soft French phrase. Despite the warmth rising from the fires and despite the steady beating of her heart, she can feel the cold, sniffing at her toe and fingertips and breathing into her coat and hair. She throws back a little of the cognac, quickly, shudderingly, then looks swiftly back at him.

'Yes.'

'Oh, well. I've long since realised that. I didn't take it personally.'

'Yes, yes, you did. You took it personally. You thought that I found you unattractive. You thought that I despised you. Didn't you?'

'No!' Megan holds his gaze, ready to be defensive; but sees he is in that fleeting state of drunkenness where one speaks the truth sometimes, without reservation, without regard for repercussions. 'Well…perhaps,' she amends, half-smiling at him, relaxing suddenly; she tips her glass again.

'Not true, not true. I was shocked, embarrassed…afraid, perhaps. You were so competent, even then. I might have made a mess of it, made a fool of myself.'

'Instead, I did.'

'I'm sorry.'

'It's okay. You don't have to apologise. Besides, you already have.'

They are sitting closely; their coat sleeves brush as Luc lifts his glass.

'You have nice cheekbones,' he says, taking up the bottle from the round table. 'We French like cheekbones. And your ears, I like those also. Small, neat, with a nice angle.' He pours a little more spirit into each of their glasses.

Megan watches his face as he does, smelling the brandy on his breath, so close she can see how the bristle of blond hairs on his chin sparkles in the candlelight, and how his eyelashes cast shadows on his skin as he looks down.

'I wonder, would you…' He hesitates, and the eyelashes come up.

His eyes are indigo and slant down slightly at the corners, and the eyelids gleam a little.

'Yes?' Say it, she thinks: say it. I'm not going to help you, not going to say it for you. I have said enough.

'Like to sleep with me tonight? It is for warmth only – of your warmth and mine I am thinking, you understand.'

Megan stares at him, frozen. And watches a slow smile twitch at the corners of his mouth, then spread into the dimple in his cheek and up to the curve of his eyes.

'Unless you would be happy for it to be otherwise.'

12

Peace

'We were going to do some work on the castles.'

'Mmm.'

They are lying on a mattress in front of the fire in the downstairs room, snugly wrapped together under layers of blanket and sleeping bag. Megan has pulled on a sweater but Luc is still naked, his body curled to her warmth, one arm under her neck, the other hand under her sweater, resting on her breast. His eyes are closed.

'The light is too dim and I don't know where my recorder is, anyway.'

'Mmm.'

'And it's too cold to get up.'

There's no reply. Luc's breathing has become regular, gently puffing against her neck.

Megan looks sideways at his sleeping face. How like children men are when they sleep, she thinks. But perhaps we are all like that when our faces are unguarded and our bodies content.

She wonders if she should get up and wash, despite the cold. Passion, like all other pleasures, has its unromantic side. But she is too comfortable, too warmly rocked by his breathing and his possessive arms to move. How do I feel about him now? she thinks. Now that I have conquered him, won back my pride? Is this an end, or a beginning? Is he simply humouring me, taking advantage of my attraction to him, or does he feel something for me?

She turns to look at him again. His face is softer: perhaps because it has filled out and his lashes are still so long, or perhaps because he's lost the intensity he had when he was younger. And his hair is short but soft – she loves the way the fringe falls forward despite its back-brushing; and he has beautiful, creamy skin, with moles only on his back. Probably in Australia those would have been cut out by now – dangerously cancerous. If he were to go back with her…

But that is perilous thinking; that path is pored with pitfalls; she pulls herself up abruptly. She turns away from his sleeping face, to look at the fire.

He had kissed her, up in the turret, gentle kisses, around her eyes, her ears, her cheekbones; then breathier, cognac kisses, hot against her neck, leaving cold patches, like ice disks, on her skin when his mouth moved away. After a while, he had unzipped her anorak and slipped a hand under layers of woollen jumper and thermal underwear until his fingertips shivered her flesh and then slowly warmed against it, moving gently, as if he were playing a piano. And later they had stumbled back to the fire and the familiarity to both of them of a double mattress. His hands had become confident as her body had responded. He had had a condom in the pocket of his greatcoat – something she not even had the wishful presentiment to think of. She was past the danger period in her cycle, but even so…

He had murmured endearments in French, repeating her name without faltering, as if it were truly a name he said often, as if he were truly aware of her as a person, not just a woman, not just as perhaps a substitute for someone else he really loved – because she knew nothing of his past women, any more than he knew of her past men. It has all, she thinks suddenly, in cold panic, happened too quickly. Too quickly…

No. Not so. A phrase from a film she saw when she was a teenager, and acutely sensitive – was it *Picnic at Hanging Rock*? – echoes in her mind: everything happens at exactly the right place and time. *Picnic at Hanging Rock* was surely about sex, too: about the impossibility of re-turning to childhood, the disappearance of the child, once the child has gained sexual awareness?

Too late for regrets, anyway. And there was no time to allow their friendship to develop in any case: he could be gone tomorrow, back to

Orléans, and she and Odette could be on the road to Spain, and she and Luc might never see each other again. Now, now that there was intimacy between them, an admitted and fulfilled desire, anything might happen: that was the beauty of sex – it was a secret passport to commitment, to instant relationship – it was as if one became blood-bound through the act, as if by mixing bodily fluids one accepted and gave adult blood-brotherhood.

She looks at the fire, at the flames flaring gold, orange, green, gas-blue: the visual and intensely beautiful manifestation of energy. If her own passion, or his, is as intense but as short-lived, then so be it, she thinks. It is all experience, all part of living, no matter what the consequences.

She rolls gently to fully face the fire and tucks her back into the curves of Luc's naked skin. She falls asleep with a drowsy contentment that infuses dreams which in the morning she doesn't remember, but which Luc sees, when he wakes briefly in the night and leans over her to put another log onto the fire, flutter smiles across her lips.

*

'Morning.'

'*Salut.*'

They look at each other, peacefully. Luc has leaned across her again to attend to the fire, so when his weight wakes her, his face is inches from her own. He brings his mouth onto hers.

'You smell of cognac.'

'Do I? Do you dislike it very much?'

'No. It's quite heady, really.'

'Huh!' He's laughing at her, breathing into her ear, his rough face brushing her neck. 'You smell of…mmm – shampoo – and…a little garlic…'

'Garlic!'

'All right, just of shampoo. It is to tease – sorry, my English is not good in the early morning – but other things are –'

'What about Odette?'

'She's in the bath. I hear the taps… I think this sweater needs to be off.'

'Absolutely necessarily?'

'*Absolument*… Ah. *Voilà. Exquises.* You don't know how these breasts haunted my dreams. All the week after you… And how they helped me through my military service. How I regretted so much not once to touch them…'

Megan is shaking her head, smiling. 'Enough,' she says. 'I see that, after all, you have become the stereotypical Frenchman. All flattery and lies.'

'And you, I see, have not changed at all. Still…*sceptique* – so un-just!'

Megan traces a finger very gently down his spine.

*

Odette, carrying Jason over her shoulder, comes down as the kettle boils. She finds the mattress neatly pushed against a wall and the fire blazing brightly, and Luc in jeans and a thick woollen jumper with his hair hanging straight and boyish and uncombed, in the kitchen making coffee.

'Good morning,' Odette says, her voice thick.

'Good morning! Are you all right? Did you sleep well? Were you warm?' Luc's eyes, a very light blue in the pale yellow sunrays angling across the stove, crease with concern as he turns to her.

'Oh, warm, yes, wonderful. And Jason only woke once. Thank you. Sorry: I just had bad dreams…' She moves to the box of foodstuffs she and Megan brought in from the van the previous night. 'Jason's starving – I've got some rice cereal here somewhere – here it is. Where's Megan?'

'She went out to the camping van to get something, and then I think she wants a bath.' He moves to a bench to the left of the stove and picks up a knife to slice the loaf of bread there; then he pauses and looks around at her. 'Odette –'

108

'Yes?'

'These bad dreams – they were not about, well, because I talked of...' He stops, frowning.

Odette has poured too much rice cereal into a bowl: she pauses from spooning the excess back into the packet. Then she suddenly smiles. 'Oh! You mean about the ghosts! No! No! My demons are not nearly so...fantastic!'

Luc nods, and picks up the knife again. 'I remember you found this castle...fearful? Is that the word?'

'Oh, yes...but that's probably just my state of mind. I'm worried about someone I have to meet again in a few days. Oh, this castle is a wonderful experience, really – and it delays...although, I suppose I want to get it over with really... Luc?'

'Yes?'

'Can I ask you something?' Odette moves over to the stove to pour boiled water onto the cereal.

'Of course.' He looks up.

'How old do you think Jason looks?'

'Jason?' Odette places the cereal bowl down and turns the little boy around. Luc looks at him carefully. 'I'm – not sure. He's not walking, so under one. Four to eight months, maybe. I'm sorry, I don't see babies –'

Odette nods; her face relaxes. 'Thanks. That's the right answer.'

Luc shrugs and turns back to cut the last slice of bread. 'I would like to ask you something, too.'

'Go ahead.' Odette sits Jason on her hip and spoons cereal into his mouth.

'Have you somewhere to stay in Alicante?'

Odette looks puzzled. 'Well, in the van, obviously. Why?'

Luc grimaces. 'I thought so. It doesn't matter.'

*

They all stand on the top step and look at the snow. Odette holds Jason in a sort of seat of her arms so he can see it too. None of them heard the fresh fall in the night. Its purity is a shock to both Megan and Odette: its whiteness is blinding in the morning sun, and almost flawless in its coverage.

'What do you think, Luc?' Megan has put on make-up and pulled her hair back, to give herself a sleek, professional look, but now her voice is uncertain.

'Well, I think the track is still clear enough. You see on the track it is not deep? Since it was cleared yesterday. I think it's okay to drive. Are you going to come with us, Odette?' He turns to her.

'No. No, I'd rather stay here, if you don't mind, and do some washing. I'll be able to dry it in front of the fire. And I should write in my diary. Jason will probably one day want to know all about this journey. I should take some photographs, too…it's such a…*primitive* place.'

'Of course. But please, stay warm, go back inside. I have brought up more firewood: use as much as you like. See you tonight, then.'

'But Megan?' Because Megan, nodding goodbye as well, has stepped down to follow him. 'Maybe you should ring that friend of Pete's again? See what's happening?' Odette has lowered her voice and there's just a tinge of reproof in it.

'Oh! Yes! I mean, if it's possible to ring long distance from somewhere… If I see a phone box, of course I will.' She's frowning, looking up at Odette. 'Only it's fairly undeveloped around here – I can't remember seeing anything…'

'Oh. But keep an eye out, won't you?'

'Do my best.' Megan smiles, and her face in the cold, pale yellow light, with her hair pulled back to reveal her sharp jawline and fine, sharp bones, looks suddenly quite beautiful. And Odette, with a jerk of agitation, thinks, she won't remember. She's so wrapped up in him, she's forgotten why we came. Or at least, why *I* did. But now, after that dream last night, I just want it over. Finished. Done.

*

'Megan, I would like to come to Spain with you.'

110

They are driving in the cherry Renault along a narrow lane in the falling twilight. Megan has been sorting her notes on her lap, and now looks up at Luc with her head tilted. All day they have moved in and out of intimacy, as if in an elaborate dance, Megan assuming a professional detachment during the interviews and photo sessions, then Luc placing his hand on her thigh or touching her face when they reached the privacy of the car again. Now she lifts the hand which rests on her knee and strokes the fingers gently with the tips of her leather gloves.

'I'd like that too,' she says slowly, 'but it wouldn't work.'

'Why?'

'There's nowhere for you to sleep, for a start.' She shudders a little from a sudden image of Luc and her cramped in the van's top bunk in the dark, each sound magnified, each movement vibrating along the walls.

'You're going to Alicante, *n'est-ce-pas*? Odette told me. There's a superb castle there. There is an elevator that lifts you through the centre of a mountain from the sea to its very heights. It was once a powerful fortress.'

'So you've been there?'

'No. But I know of it. My interest is in history, remember.' He has to lift his hand from hers to change gear.

'Not music, songs, so much any more?' Megan's voice softens.

'Yes, that too. In Paris, I play with a band in a cave – you know what it is?'

'Mmm, a sort of small nightclub. What kind of music do you play?'

'American songs mainly. Some of mine at the end. But American songs are the most popular. You could come…' He glances at her, then back at the road.

Megan is silent for a moment. Then she says, 'It's not that I don't want you to come to Spain with us. But think of it: how would Odette feel? And it's very important, this interview – the purpose of our whole trip.' She fiddles with her gloves, plucking at the fingers and stretching them slightly. 'Plus, we have to get visas at the border – I don't know if you need one too. And we'll have to stop overnight, maybe two or three.' She looks at him, but the road is winding and he has to concentrate on it.

It is a moment before he says, 'What about after Odette goes home? After the interview? She will be able to take a plane from Alicante to connect, *n'est-ce pas?* Perhaps I could come then. We could hire a room? I have ten days of my vacation left.'

Megan, still looking at his profile, shakes her head slightly. It's impossible, of course it's impossible: it might even take longer than a week to find Dickson if they're unlucky, and then she has to get the van back to Paris…but wouldn't it have been nice, so nice, if they could have done that: had a real holiday, exploring the old city, making love in a Spanish bed, eating out at restaurants late into the nights, dancing perhaps, walking on the white sand on the edge of the Mediterranean with the shadow of the vast fortress etched perhaps on the water…

'Well, we'll work something out,' she says, softly.

*

Of course, it won't last, this happiness, Megan thinks. And yet, as she huddles in a cocoon of blankets and zipped-out sleeping bag beside Luc, and she watches him bend over the fire, his shoulders hunched under the greatcoat, his hands competent and swift, his hair golden against the light, she observes her own tenderness with amusement. What is it about him, she thinks, which makes me feel such desire?

'You must have a girlfriend. Two, three. I refuse to believe you don't.'

He is facing the fire, and manipulates a heavy log into place before looking over his shoulder to answer. His expression is serious. 'There was a girl I thought I would marry, eventually, but she met someone else. A better musician.' A slight edge of sarcasm, something she hasn't heard in his voice before, tinges the last sentence; he turns back to the flames. 'When she wanted to come back to me, it was too late. And others, short affairs. Is that the word? But I teach at a Catholic school: it is necessary to be discreet. And it is hard to meet the right one, the one who will like you as well, don't you think?'

Megan doesn't answer. She waits until he turns his back on the fire and leans on his heels facing her. She says then, softly, 'Yes. But I've never met anyone I thought I could marry. I mean, I've met lots of men I'm attracted to, I've had affairs, if you want to call them that, but no one I've wanted to spend the rest of my life with.'

He's looking at her, frowning, his expression inscrutable.

So she says quickly, 'You must think that's terribly promiscuous. That I'm a slut, even?'

'Oh, Megan –'

'Do you?'

He looks at her quietly. 'No, no I do not. I find you…honest. We are both adults, we are not religious. Such words are for children and the – *pieux* – pious?'

Megan smiles then and throws back her head, her hands clasped beneath her chin with her elbows on her drawn-up knees. 'Oh, my,' she says, looking at him with slanted, teasing eyes, 'You are schooled well! How beautifully you put it. Well, it doesn't really matter whether you do believe that or not: I think you like me a little, either way. I like you. Even if I thought you were a slut, I'd still like you. So there you are.'

'Ah.' He puts his head on one side and regards her seriously. 'You see? We think alike. This is why I must come to Spain to be with you.'

'Well, I've been thinking about that.' Megan watches him carefully then. It might be all very well for him to have a brief little fling with her in the anonymity of this castle and a private room in a foreign city, but how willing might he be to have her come into his real life in Paris? 'Today's Thursday. I have to have the van back to Paris by Saturday next week. It's possible Odette may be able to leave in a few days, but I don't think it's very probable. I wondered if perhaps, well, you see, I have to come back to Paris anyway… And you did mention playing in a band. I'd like to hear you.'

'You would rather have some days with me in Paris?' He has raised his eyebrows.

'Well, it would be more practical.'

'But not so nice, perhaps…my apartment is not large, and Paris is very cold right now.'

'Yes.' Megan drops her head and hugs her knees more tightly. 'Oh, well, it was just a thought… I can ring you, anyway, if you give me a number, and there might be a few days after Odette goes…' Her voice is a little muffled.

'Megan?'

'Mmm?'

Luc waits until she raises her head again. 'I would like to come to Spain, but if it is not possible, then you must come to me in Paris. Okay? I want to see you again.'

Megan looks at him levelly. 'Me too,' she says.

He hesitates, holding her gaze – then suddenly smiles. 'Good. It's settled.' He pushes back on his heels. 'Now it's late, and we should go to the castle of M. Dumaurier early tomorrow so you can be in Spain before the night. It is warmer, tonight, don't you think – perhaps you will not need to sleep in your sweater?' He raises one eyebrow quizzically as he finishes, then stands up so she can see the nakedness of his body inside the greatcoat.

13

Cerbère

It is almost dusk when the mustard van pulls into a campsite three kilometres from the outskirts of Cerbère, a French town bordering the Spanish coast. The campsite is simply a long snaking road cut in terraces into a cliff, winding down to the Mediterranean: there are only three other vehicles parked on it. No one comes out to greet or direct them.

Megan hesitates, then trundles the van down the slope to the lowest loop of the road. She parks with the nose of the van angled out to sea. 'We might as well have a view,' she says, feigning optimism, as the engine shudders to a stop.

Odette takes Jason down to the sea while Megan goes to find a caretaker. She carries her baby clumsily down a rough track to a pebble cove. The air is heavy and tangy with salt, cold, but at least five degrees warmer than it was inland. She places him on a patch of sand and he seizes with delight everything within reach – broken driftwood, milky pebbles and opaque coins of glass. She looks towards Spain. The Mediterranean rushes blackly and peacefully at the edges of the Pyrenees in the thickening light, and on the mountainside the white and yellow lights of Cerbère are beginning to glimmer. The surrounding hills, terraced with vineyards, are like an old ribbed brown jumper.

On one of the loops of the campsite road she sees two shy lovers, grey-haired, walking slowly arm in arm towards a caravan. Both their caravan and the other two vehicles huddle parallel to the cliff side. She looks up uneasily at her own van, its nose courageously, or stupidly, pointed to the sea.

'Bad news, I'm afraid,' says Megan, when Odette joins her back in the cabin. She's bent over a map at the table, a glass of cognac beside her. Ever since they left Luc, after a quick roadside lunch outside the grounds of M. Dumaurier's castle – which Megan had photographed and taken notes on with admirable efficiency – waving as he turned right at a crossroads and they left, she's been quiet.

Odette, interpreting the silence correctly as Megan's adjustment back to her professional self, to her honing of her concentration to the task ahead – the sort of concentration which won her the job of chasing Odette's story in the first place – doesn't comment on the silence.

'Only cold showers, and twenty-five dollars a night. And he reckons there won't be anybody to buy a visa from at the border tomorrow. Because it's New Year's Eve, the guards will be on holiday.'

'Does it really matter if we don't have visas then?'

'I don't know. They're supposed to be fifty dollars each, including Jason. It's a fair bit, so we might get into trouble later, if we get caught.'

'Perhaps we won't need to show our passports, though, if there's no one at the border, and going back into France you should only have to see French customs people…'

'Mmm, but they sometimes want to see them at camping grounds.'

'That's true.'

A sudden gust of wind shakes the van, and they both glance up at the southern cabin window, but they can see little through the lace and opaque glass except a black rump of sea cliff and above it the lights of Cerbère.

'All the other caravans are facing north.' Odette's voice is carefully casual.

'Mmm. The caretaker pointed that out to me too but he just shrugged when I asked if we should do the same. I don't know. Be nice to wake up to that view in the morning.'

'Does he think there's going to be a storm?'

'No – at least, he didn't say anything about one. Oh look, let's have something to eat. I'm starving. If a wind springs up, we can always move then. But it's really so calm – I can't imagine it suddenly blowing up a gale if it's so calm now.'

'Jason's pretty hungry too, aren't you, sweetheart? He's beginning to eat more and more. Okay. At least it's not so cold. What have we got?'

'Not sure – don't think there's much, though. We'll have to do a shop tomorrow. God, I hope not everyone in Spain will be on holiday because it's New Year's Eve. Shouldn't be, though, surely. Spain should be cheaper than France – it used to be – so it'll be better if we can go straight over and find a supermarket there. There's some tinned stuff in the cupboard for now, though, I think – ravioli? That's it. And some lettuce and capsicum, I think.'

What does it matter about taking care with food any more? Megan thinks. Now there's no Luc to impress. She drains her glass and pours another, watching Odette clamp on the tin opener.

*

It is just after Odette has settled Jason and they are both preparing for bed that the wind comes up in earnest. At first, it only gently shakes the van; then over the next half-hour, as Megan studies a road map up in her bunk and Odette sorts through clothes for Jason and herself for the next day, it begins to whistle around the windows and thump intermittently against the glass. Then suddenly a gust flings against the southern-facing side and the whole van shudders and seems almost to lift.

Odette looks up in real alarm and Megan's head comes out over the edge of the upper bunk. And there is another great thump against the van.

'I don't like the sound of that. Damn. We're going to have to move after all. Damn, damn, damn.' Megan's legs swing over the edge of the bunk and she lowers herself expertly, being careful to avoid the sleeping Jason. 'This is going to wake Jason again, isn't it? The engine makes such a bloody racket, and we'll have to have everything turned off. Why didn't I just move before?'

But Odette doesn't respond: her eyes are large and dark.

There's another violent buffet against the van.

117

'It's going to take at least five minutes to warm up the engine.' And, against all rationality, Megan thinks, why couldn't Luc be here? The bloody caretaker wouldn't have been so smug if Luc had been with us – would have been more honest. Probably thinks we're English.

She feels tired suddenly: tired of coping, tired of making decisions. Tired of being strong. She finds the keys and, without looking at the silent Odette, flings open the back door and stumbles out.

The wind makes her gasp. It has become a steady stream, like water flowing, cold and strong and relentless. It whips at her hair and coat as she fumbles to turn off the gas tap in the dark; it stings her eyes as she turns then to the driver door. She glances down, over the cliff edge only metres away from the nose of the van, at the Mediterranean. Black, foaming waves tear jaggedly at the rocks below: the sea is a writhing mass of glistening threats. She opens the door grimly and it slams shut after her.

The engine seems to take an age to start. It turns, labours, stops. The wind rocks the van and she looks through the windscreen at the sucking water into which they would be thrown if the van should over-turn.

At last, it roars into life. She takes a deep breath and clicks the gear into reverse. Jerkily, she backs and turns. But which way to position the van, so that it is buffeted the least? She's not sure. She tries one angle: the van lurches alarmingly. Hastily, she reverses – then in panic shoves on the brake. Her rear vision is blind. Eventually, taking deep breaths, trying to be logical, she decides that the back should take the most pressure, so angles it again, but this time with the nose into the cliff wall.

She idles the engine and closes her eyes. Her fear is real, verging on panic, but she is reluctant to recognise that. The van shudders again, but this time without a sideways kick: shudders again, but not violently. She opens her eyes, nods and switches off the motor. God, she thinks, I should have got Odette and Jason out before I moved. What if we'd gone over? She shudders herself at the thought.

Jason has woken, but is only whingeing half-heartedly as Odette shushes him on her shoulder. Megan grimaces as she pushes open the grey velveteen curtains which separate the cockpit from the cabin; she can tell from Odette's drawn face and wide eyes that Odette too was aware of their danger.

'You okay?'

'Yeah.'

'Oh, God, stupid. I was stupid not to move when the caretaker pointed out those other vans! I should have realised…sorry.'

Odette pats the quieting Jason rhythmically, rocking her body. 'It did…seem strange –'

But Megan cuts her off, jerking her head up. 'It's just – I hate the way men do that, you know? The arrogance. She thinks she knows what she's doing: I'll show her how wrong she is. That men are cleverer. That they should listen to us, to our subtleties, because we know best. Bloody hell. What would he have done if we'd ended up going over the edge?'

Odette stares, shakes her head, then closes her eyes, gripping Jason.

And Megan stares back. 'Well…it probably wasn't as dangerous as all that,' she says, more steadily. 'The van's pretty heavy. It felt dangerous, but it probably wasn't.'

Odette's eyes are still shut. 'Maybe.'

And Megan's mouth drops open in surprise. Shit, she thinks. What's getting into her?

*

The wind shakes the van all night: both Megan and Odette wake intermittently to its gusts. Odette lies in the darkness of two o'clock thinking, it's all right, the worst that can happen now is that the van tips and wedges against the cliff. But she keeps Jason close to her body, one arm protectively around him. Perhaps because of this he wakes and wants to be breastfed back to sleep three times in the night. Megan thinks, I'm sick of it: sick of dealing with arrogant men. That's all I encounter in this job. What should we do tomorrow? If we can't get visas? Bet the bloody guards'll be as helpful as hyenas. What if we can't buy food because it's a holiday? What if Dickson has disappeared and this whole trip is fruitless?

What if Luc has someone else in Paris?

In the morning, it is nine o'clock before any of the three stir: to find that the wind has gone, but floating in the shallows of the sea is a mustard-coloured tarpaulin, the same shade as their van. Odette and Megan look at it silently.

As Megan drives the van out, the caretaker hales them. He has been sloshing out the toilet block: he carries a tin pail and a straw-brush broom and smells of disinfectant. In French, he says, 'Thought you'd landed in the drink! Good to see you're still with us!'

'Thanks for your help,' says Megan, dryly.

They drive below the terraced hills of Cerbère to the Spanish border, and find only Frenchmen guarding the entrance to France there, as the caretaker of the camping ground predicted; the Spanish frontier is unmanned.

'Les Espagnols,' a guard says, when Megan approaches them for advice, 'ils sont paresseux, eux!' The Spanish are lazy. They shrug and indicate with their heads that Megan should simply pass.

And so, on the last day of the year, the three cross the frontier into Spain.

14

Lianca

So this is Spain, Odette thinks. Spain. Land of flamenco dancing, of lace fans flicked open with strong brown fingers; Hemingway's Spain: of handsome tanned faces chin-tilted proudly under black boleros, of bullfighting – of masculine courage pitted against the terror of instinct – and clean, pure fishing in mountain streams and wine-skins passed from hand to hand and a simplicity of life where men have their place and women have no part in it, but flutter uneasily at the edges of male consciousness nevertheless, like giant caged exotic moths which if released have the power to castrate a man.

Hemingway. She had read *Fiesta* and a number of his short stories in first year university: her tutor had loved his writing passionately, but hated his politics. The images of Spain remained for Odette because of that: seemed to clothe the country in a raiment of romanticism tinged with dangerous morality.

Or had remained. It was what had tipped the balance more than Megan's urging for her to come on this trip: to think, some of this might be exciting, exotic – a world of difference from Biloela and Rockhampton and a landscape of grey-green trees and broad, dry streets. But as they trundle past the deserted passport-check booths, past the closed currency exchange windows, and nose toward a narrow cliff road, she feels a weight of depression dragging on her, like the sensation of heaviness induced by sitting in a draining bath.

It's the broken sleep and the night's worry, she thinks, shaking herself. It's these dreams I've been having about Dickson, the smell of him, greasy, oily, like fish, oily fish. It all seemed so real – him in the van with me, standing over me, breathing on me with his hot, fishy breath...

And it's the scare last night… I should have been more assertive, made Megan move the van earlier, trusted my instincts. She takes a breath, lifting her chin and squaring her shoulders. But we're here now, we're in Spain. And it will be beautiful, romantic, compensate for the cold and fear and loneliness…having to face him again…

But Portbou, the Spanish border village, is unadorned and quiet and disappointingly domestic: the only people they see are two young girls dressed in heavy coats and beanies, their feet tramping heavily along the narrow road.

*

'Think we'll drive down the coast road to Lianca, then take a red road to Gerona,' says Megan, drawing Odette's attention back to the map on the dashboard. 'The yellow roads – the *autopista* – are toll roads, I think. Luc said they're expensive. The red roads are free and almost as direct, by the looks. We'll try to get some money at Lianca. I doubt they'd have an ATM that accepts MasterCard in this little town. Lianca looks a lot bigger. If I can get change, I'll ring Pete from there too – he'll want to know how we're going – and the contact in Alicante, Jerome. We should look out for a supermarket as well.'

They are already on the southern outskirts of Portbou anyway.

The mountains to the south are snow-wrapped and in places clothed in cloud. Against the windswept, blank sky, the clean edges of the mountains look as if they are superimposed film, clipped onto a false backdrop. Odette's heart lifts a little at the purity of the lines. But then she looks down, as they round a bend, and almost gasps at the closeness of the road to cliffs which are a sheer drop down to a seething Mediterranean. Megan, driving the right-hand drive vehicle on the inside lane on the right, doesn't seem to notice either the road's danger or Odette's nervousness.

It takes them an hour to reach Lianca, even though it is only twenty kilometres away on the map. The map doesn't show how treacherous the mountain road is. By the time they pull up in the town centre, which borders the sea, it is nearly lunchtime and Megan is cranky and cursing. Jason is hungry but not demandingly so: Odette is able to divert his attention with a noisy rattle when she's clambered out of the van; and then the distractions of people around him calm him temporarily. Odette herself is carefully quiet.

They wander among lunchtime crowds and eventually find an ATM.

Megan takes out money with relief, then turns to hand some to Odette. 'How about you buy some bread and cheese – tomatoes if you can find some? There are roughly a hundred pesetas to the dollar – easy, isn't it? Mind you, last time I was in Spain I got more like a hundred and fifty. Now, I have to ring Pete – he'll think we're dead or something. Besides, he may have made some headway getting those other women Dickson harassed to go public – wouldn't that make a difference? And I'll never get through tomorrow, it being a public holiday. He's probably going to have a nice drunken lunch with his family – swim in the pool to sober up and a sleep under the mango tree to wear off the sleep debt of New Year's Eve celebrations. Oh, shit.'

'What?' Odette, folding the notes, looks up.

'New Year's Eve. They're ten hours ahead of us. It's nearly ten o'clock in Brisbane. There's no way I'll be able to catch him: he'll be out partying for sure. Damn.' She looks at Odette uneasily: she is aware of Odette's depression, and the need to lift it in this last, crucial phase of their journey. Good news about Dickson's other victims could do that.

Odette shrugs. 'It's no big deal. It's more important to get through to Jerome – is that how you pronounce it? – isn't it?'

'Well, yes, of course.' Jason has dropped his rattle: Megan watches Odette bend to pick it up. 'Okay. I'll try Pete at home tonight at…ten p.m. – eight tomorrow morning his time. Too bad if he's sleeping in. And Jerome should be in for lunch now, if he's adapted to Spanish habits, so I might be lucky and catch him – and he might have heard from Pete anyway.'

She lifts her head then, brisk again. 'Now, you get something to eat

– something to make sandwiches with. Then go down to the beach, the end of this street here. See, there're benches on the sand. In the sun. I'll meet you there. Okay?'

Odette nods, pocketing the money. At the mention of food, she is conscious of a gnawing hunger – they ate little for breakfast – and Jason too seems to react the words: he begins to whinge again. 'He wants a feed. See you soon.' For a moment, she stands absently hushing Jason, watching Megan until she is lost in the crowd. Then she turns slowly and looks around.

Across the street, which is narrow and busy, there seem to be some sorts of food shops. They each have brightly coloured awnings, in contrasting colours to the adjacent shop, with words, in Spanish of course, printed on their windows. And she's suddenly frozen, her limbs paralysed. How can I do this? she thinks. I can't speak the language, not a word of it. I can't do it, I can't.

She stands very still, until Jason begins to squirm and cry. Then she thinks, all I have to do is point. Bread and cheese, tomatoes and oranges perhaps. And something to drink. She begins to cross the road, pushing down her fear. And from the middle of the road sees metal grilles gently descending over shop windows all along the street. 'No!' she cries aloud: 'What's happening?' It's the middle of the day… Why should everything be closing? She looks in confusion up and down the suddenly deserted street, and sees one doorway still open: a bakery.

A stout woman is wiping down the glass-topped bench above empty shelves.

'Uh – bread?' she stammers, pointing to a lone loaf in a wire basket behind the woman.

The woman looks at her with firmly pressed lips and seems about to refuse; then Jason begins to cry again and she relents. She wraps thin paper around the loaf and hands it over, holding out her other palm. Odette fumbles in her pocket for the money Megan gave her and hastily hands over a crumpled note. The woman returns change from her apron, but only closes her eyes and nods at Odette's hesitant 'Thank you.'

The bakery door shuts behind Odette as she leaves.

The beach is only a short walk away, but Jason has progressed to insistent howls by the time she reaches it. She settles him hastily to her breast on the sunny, if wind-chilled, beach bench and clumsily pulls off a chunk of the bread over his bulky clothing. Crumbs from the thick crust fall on him as she eats it and he clutches at them as he sucks. She chews miserably: the bread is dry and she's perhaps even more thirsty than hungry. I should have tried to buy something to drink, she thinks; but she had not seen anything in the bakery except that one loaf, and she had lacked the courage to ask for anything more.

She munches on disconsolately, staring about her. Around a fishing boat out on the water, seagulls swarm like flies. The sand is surprisingly white, in a flat strip between two rocky outcrops. A middle-aged couple in jeans and long woollen jumpers stroll along the water's edge, their arms around each other. There is a plate-glassed restaurant built on the sand's edge to her right: she watches the diners furtively from time to time. They seem animated – there are bottles of wine on every table – and the restaurant is full. She thinks, it's New Year's Eve. If I were here on a holiday with Matt and we had money, we could eat in there, three or four courses, and sleep all afternoon while Jason did; then go out tonight – see in the New Year properly…

We haven't got much money left. I didn't have much to put in to start with, and I know Megan's way over the budget she predicted in Australia.

Australia. If I were at home now, what would I be doing? Be at Mum's, probably, lying by the pool, getting a suntan, reading a book while Jason has his sleep. Everyone pretending Matt's not in jail. Then tonight I'd go out with my sisters and their husbands and they'd all boost me up. Tell me they support me. That it could have happened to anyone – to one of them.

Then she thinks, no, no, that's not right. It's night there now. It's ten o'clock. She sighs.

She has just changed Jason's nappy, much to his objection at the still chill air, and dumped the soiled one, with an apologetic grimace to nothing in particular, into an adjoining rubbish bin when Megan joins her.

'How'd you go?'

'I couldn't get anything except bread. Everywhere suddenly shut.'

'Oh, shit.' Megan plonks down on the bench. 'Shit. I forgot about that. Siesta. Everything closes from midday till two or three. Shit.'

'How did you go?' Odette's voice is absently polite. Then, before Megan can answer, she adds, 'Can you hold Jason for a minute? There's a drinking fountain over there and I want to wash my hands and get a drink. Thanks.'

Megan takes Jason in surprise. She sits on the bench holding him, frowning, until he burps suddenly; and her face relaxes into a smile at him, which he returns, waving his arms around.

'Well?' says Odette when she returns.

Megan passes Jason to her outstretched arms, patting him gently on a cheek as she does so. 'Did I get through, do you mean? Mmm. Do you want the good news or the bad news first?'

But Odette only looks at her silently, lowering herself onto the bench.

'Okay. The good. Dickson is staying with his relatives at last: been there since Wednesday, apparently. And the house he's staying in is cramped, so he's not there much – spends a lot of time wandering around the city. Which is going to give us the opportunity to surprise him.' Megan pauses, leaning back and linking her fingers together in her lap.

'The bad news is that Jerome wants us to hold off a little. Maybe three days. He wants to see what sort of routine Dickson develops. He's a methodical man, remember: likes his daily patterns…' She breaks off, cursing herself silently: Odette's memory of those patterns is of course not at all pleasant.

'Has he heard from Pete?' Odette lowers Jason to the sand and play-walks him around her feet, with her back straight and her arms stiff and strong.

Jason flicks his yellow-socked feet in the sand and bounces on them tentatively under his mother's support. His eyes are wide with excitement and he chuckles, his cheeks pink from the cold wind. She coos back automatically but doesn't smile.

'Well – yes. No go with the other women. At least, yet.' She gets it out quickly and looks at Odette sideways.

Odette seems occupied with her bouncing child: she doesn't reply for a moment. Then, her voice thick, she says, 'He'll be crawling soon. He's already sitting up so well.'

Megan glances from the baby to Odette, calculatingly; then she asks, gently, 'How old is he now?'

Odette keeps her face still in profile. 'Six months.'

Megan can barely hear her. 'Is that when they normally start to sit?'

'Mmm.'

'He's a nice little baby.'

Odette's head shifts slightly toward Megan, but she doesn't look up. 'He's pretty good.'

'Well, he wakes you up a bit, but he's still a nice little baby. Sweet-natured – I don't hear him cry much. Doesn't whinge. I hate whingeing children.'

'Well, they probably have their reasons. They just respond to their environment, after all. But I'm glad he isn't, too.' Odette's voice sounds more normal. 'There's the bread, if you want some. It's pretty dry, but it's better than nothing.'

'I...thanks.' Megan breaks a piece off and takes a small bite. There's a silence while she swallows it and takes another.

Then Odette, taking a deep breath and sitting up straight and turning her body, says, 'Megan?'

'Mmm?'

'I've been thinking. I've had lots of time to think, waking up so much, you know. I'm wondering if we should just forget about this. Pull the pin. You could go back, spend your holiday with Luc. I could fly out, tomorrow even, from Barcelona?'

Jason has been dancing around her feet as she speaks, straining on her arms; now she crosses her hands to make him turn and lets him flop onto the sand, supporting his back in a 'V' with her feet so he can't fall sideways and hit his head on the edge of the cemented pebble platform on which the bench sits.

She wraps her arms around her body and hunches it again. 'I…I've been dreaming about him. Nightmares. The thought of seeing him again – bringing it all back… I don't know if I can do it. I'm…sorry.'

'What?'

'I'm sorry. Maybe it's the strain of last night – that terrible wind – and not much sleep and then that *drive* this morning – so treacherous! – and the visas. Now not being able to buy food. It's like a series of omens, all of it. And I don't want any more of it. It's not worth it. What can we achieve? What can I achieve? It's not worth it.' Odette's eyes are imploring.

Megan has finished the piece of bread; she brushes crumbs off her jeans slowly, sitting up straight, only her head turned to Odette. 'Okay.' She rests her hands on either side of her on the bench and her voice is low and reasoned. 'Okay. You could do that. I could do that. We could just leave it and forget about it and go back to our separate lives. Matt will be out of prison in four and a half months and you two can move in together and pretend none of it happened. Dickson can get away with it scot-free, live on here in Spain in luxury, never have to atone for his…*cruelty*. Pal up with Christopher Skase, perhaps – two of a kind really…'

'All right. All right, Megan, I know. I'm the one who was… It was me, it was me, you remember?' She drops her head then into her hands, holding her forehead with cold fingers, feeling the sharp pain across her shoulders from the strain of having Jason strapped to her chest so often. 'But I've had enough of this – enough! The cold, the worry of having to face him again – I can't go through with it, I don't think I can go through with it, I'll mess it up, I know, or else it won't do any good, it'll be useless.' She has begun to cry.

Megan stares at Odette's thin hunched shoulders. She thinks, yes, oh yes, it would be so easy. Phone Luc, book somewhere on the edge of the Mediterranean and to hell with the expense. Eat, drink and be merry. As Dickson probably is. Then go back, or perhaps not go back, with the castle story. Leave Odette to her nightmares.

She looks back at the beach. The waves wash rhythmically in little tame curls onto the flat sand. The sun shines from a harmless sky.

'No.'

Odette is searching for a tissue in her coat pocket: she blows her nose and wipes her eyes and says through the thin paper, 'Why not?'

'Because it's cowardly.'

'Cowardly? Cowardly? I let that man, that fat, sickening, pig of a man, do those things to me – oh, God, have you any idea? I'm not a coward.'

'I didn't say you were a coward, 'Dette.' Megan's voice is soft now, soft and measured and thoughtful and she's looking at the sea. 'Just that to leave now would be cowardly. That's how the men would see it. Pete, Dickson if he found out, perhaps your Matt. I don't know. But it's Dickson who's the coward. He's run away because he can't, or won't, face consequences. He took advantage of you, of you loving Matt. He's stolen thousands from the taxpayer. He's brutal and selfish and arrogant – but only to the vulnerable. It's Dickson who is the true coward. We have to make him see that.'

Odette has been sitting with her arms folded and her tear-streaked face turned to the glass walls of the beach restaurant, her hair long and straight and black like a swift brushstroke on the pale clear beauty of her profile. She turns her head back now to Megan. 'It's all right for you,' she says. Her voice is harsh. 'What can happen to you?'

'Nothing's going to happen to you, Odette. Nothing.' Megan's voice is very gentle. 'But maybe something will happen to him. If we can do this, get it right, maybe we can blow him right out of his hiding hole into front-page news. And get Matt out of prison.'

'And make you a star? Ace reporter?'

Megan lifts an eyebrow then, and one side of her mouth twitches into a smile. 'You think I'm doing this for me, don't you?'

'Aren't you?'

Jason has lurched over onto his front: his crawling movements are crushing sand into the creases of his sleeves and under his wristbands. Odette squats to pick him up.

Megan watches Odette's swift movements, the way she deftly flicks sand out from under Jason's wrists and brushes his hands together and smooths his fleecy all-in-one tracksuit all the way down to its thick-socked toes. 'To some degree,' she replies, her voice still soft. 'Of course. Yes, of course I am. But I have reason to hate Dickson as well, you know. Or at least to loathe him. Reason to want to see him brought down.'

'What? What's he done to you?'

Megan hesitates. She flinches still at the memory: her in his office, trying to get a statement, the way he sat behind his desk, his feet on it, shoes shining, eyes glinting, screwing up the pages one by one and throwing them at her, at her breasts, first one side then the other. Talking, talking, his voice more and more measured, more and more menacing. Smiling his wet-lipped smile. Screwing up the pages of the copy of Odette's report. While she had sat quite still with one hand clenching a biro and the other a notepad.

'Oh, nothing compared to what he did to you. Just humiliation stuff. But enough to make me loathe him. *Loathe* him.'

She sees Odette is calming. Jason is cuddled in her lap again and her lips are closed and still. Megan is quiet for a moment, looking down. Then she says gently, 'Dickson thinks he's safe in Spain. He thinks because he has Spanish citizenship no one can touch him. But if we can get this tape – him admitting his blackmail of you, admitting he planted that dope on Matt because you refused to let him rape you a second time, maybe even admitting he assaulted those other girls – and splash that all over the front page of a national newspaper, we'll have enough evidence to force an external investigation into him. We'll see how far the 'internal investigators' can cover things up then.'

They are silent, staring at each other. Then Megan says, 'Four days, Odette. Four more days. And it'll get better, I promise. And then we'll get him.'

15

Tossa de Mar

Back in the van, Megan warms tinned beef, and they eat that with the rest of the bread, washing it down with strong coffee. Then they clean up with water heated with the last of the gas, strap themselves into their seats again and head out of Lianca on the N260, inland, towards Gerona.

'"Few travellers know what they're missing when, on their way from Barcelona to France, they bypass the stone alleyways of Gerona,"' Odette reads aloud over Jason's sleeping head from the 1993 *Let's Go Europe* some previous hirer of the camper van has left in the glove box. Her voice is a little dreamy.

Megan glances at her and Odette half-grimaces, half-smiles.

'But we're heading in the wrong direction, anyway,' Odette says.

Megan smiles at the road. 'So you are interested in some of this journey, aren't you? Despite having Dickson at the end of it?'

'It's partly why I agreed to come.' Odette has lowered the book. 'I've had this thing about Spain since I was at school... I don't know, it appealed to my imagination or something.'

'Yeah?' Megan glances sideways again. She is quiet for a moment. She has a strong desire to drive straight through to Alicante, driving overnight, even; and once there, to set up in a camping ground, orientate herself, and wait. But really, there is no urgent need to. And they have to stop somewhere soon anyway to get camping gas and food. And Odette was so good about those two days in Luc's castle: it might compensate...

She says slowly, 'Odette, you know how Jerome doesn't want us to approach Dickson for a few more days? Well, I was thinking – maybe we could slow this trip down a bit. I don't mean stop in a big place like Gerona, but maybe at a picturesque little town on the coast. Or at different places for one night each. We could ring Jerome from each and get an update.'

'Well, I...' Odette's voice peters out.

Megan takes a breath. 'Tell you what. You read up on what there is to see. I want to basically follow the red road down the coast – it'll be warmer near the sea and it's pretty direct as well – but if there are nice places to stop, then why shouldn't we?'

Odette purses her lips, her head turned to the window; then she lifts the book again. When she answers, her voice flickers slightly with excitement. 'I suppose you're right. Since we're going to have to wait anyway.' She shifts Jason to a more comfortable position and props a road map of Spain behind the book.

After a while, she reads aloud, '"Tossa de Mar is a blissful resort on the lower part of the Costa Brava, about forty kilometres north of Barcelona...the chief lure is the Vila Vella (old town), a collection of fourteenth- and fifteenth-century buildings and fortifications on the rocky peninsula by the beach." It's not really very far from here, but I if we could get food and things in a little place like that today, tomorrow we could bypass Barcelona and stop tomorrow night somewhere on the Costa Dorada, then go down as far perhaps as Valencia, then the next day arrive in Alicante?'

Megan hides a smile by dropping her head forward so her wedge of hair obscures her cheek. She tries to shrug nonchalantly. 'You don't want to stop in Barcelona?'

Odette looks at the big yellow blob of Barcelona on the map, and shakes her head. 'I don't think so. I know it's an artistic centre and everything, but it's got three million people in it and it doesn't even look as if it's ten kilometres in diameter. After London...'

Megan whistles. 'Point taken. We could get lost and never get out. All right. Tossa de Mar it is.' She mentally gives herself the thumbs up.

*

They follow the N11 past Gerona, then head down towards the coast. Near Malgrat de Mar, they turn from the highway and take a minor road to backtrack the twenty kilometres or so to Tossa. And Odette feels her heightened spirits begin to sink. For the Costa Brava, the Brave Coast, rugged and romantic in her imagination, is a forest only of high-rise buildings, cluttered together in ugly blocks, right up to the edge of a flat, dirty beach. Wind gusts along the narrow, busy coast road in grey-dusted billows.

They pass a series of seaside towns as cramped together as suburbs in a city, until eventually the road begins to climb; then the coast is rugged and wild – but only in a way that lurches Odette's heart instead of lifting it. And then they come to Tossa de Mar.

They follow the road all the way down to the sea and stop down near a beach, parking easily in a winter-deserted beachfront car park. Then Odette, with Jason blinking from sleep, climbs out of the van, and she turns with Megan to look at the town.

And both of them are arrested, as if spellbound. For behind a modern facade of bright shopfronts, the old town seems as hand-built and natural as a child's sandcastle, rising as it does in exactly the same colours as the sand in which it stands. Its streets are narrow and uneven, as if carved out by a childish hand, and only the glint of glass in window frames and patches of bright cloth on lines strung across the streets lend it reality.

It's three o'clock.

'Well, this is nice, isn't it?' Megan grimaces at her own inarticulation, so hurries on, 'I'm going to empty the port-a-pottee in those toilets. Discreetly. I completely forgot about it this morning at Cerbère – too keen to get out of the place. Do you want to look around and see if you can find some sort of convenience store – one that sells gas, particularly?'

Odette breathes in the cold sea air sharply and drags her attention away from the enchanted town, then realises what Megan has asked. 'I – well, I guess so.' The memory of her last attempt at shopping flutters uneasily in her belly.

But this time, to her relief, it is as simple as shopping for the Christmas food had been. One of the shops on the seafront is a mini-super-market. She takes a red plastic basket with wire handles and works out from the label photographs what she needs to buy. There is a deli section with pre-packaged cheeses and meats. Near the checkout there are bottles of wine and a basket of different shaped and textured breads, and – such luck! – a stand of blue gas canisters, for only four hundred pesetas each. She places her purchases and her empty gas canister on the counter beside a full one, then indicates that she wants to swap the used for the new; and when the checkout girl rattles off the total, all Odette has to do is look at the electronic digits on the cash register and hand over a two-thousand-peseta note.

Megan is waiting at the van, and they pack the purchases away together; then Odette feeds Jason while Megan searches in the *Let's Go Europe* for the closest open camping ground, but none is listed.

'Well,' she says eventually, 'I guess what we should do is try to find some sort of information bureau now – it's a tourist resort after all. It's got to have an information office and camping grounds somewhere – and then we can have a look around the old town, if you like.'

They scan the seafront together and come across a large blue 'i' above an arrow quite quickly; but when they find the information centre, a sign tells them in English that it is closed until May; bars and restaurants near the beach, obviously catering for tourists, are all closed as well. Despondently, they wander back to the van.

'Perhaps if we drive to the outskirts of the town, we'll see a camping ground sign?' Odette's voice has an optimism she doesn't feel. She realises suddenly that she had wanted, in coming to so obvious a tourist attraction on New Year's Eve, to not only experience the uniqueness of the town, but also to possibly make contact with other English-speakers, to see the New Year in with them and not just Megan – to relieve, if only briefly, the pressure of their journey's quest, to pretend she was only a tourist, and to delight in the foreignness of the country as any other tourist might. Now it seems that that possibility is remote.

'Well…I don't really want to move the van again until I have to. So let's have a look at the old town first, and then we can do that. But if we can't find a campsite, we'll have to free camp. I don't really want to tackle that coast road again in the dark.'

So it begins to seem for both of them as if the Vila Vella is spoiled. For despite the fact that they have gas again, and fresh food and wine, the spectre of no showers and a night worrying about their vulnerability in not having the protection of a camping ground depresses Megan. Particularly because it is New Year's Eve, and she, too, was anticipating a carefree night. Which, she can't help thinking, would have been the case if they'd driven straight through to Alicante, despite arriving late at night: there would certainly be open campsites in a major city.

So, each suppressing her disappointment, they begin to wander dutifully among the cobbled streets. But then gradually, as they touch the ancient walls and trace with their eyes the patterns in wrought-iron balconies, as they listen absently to rough Spanish voices chattering and calling, and to the occasional strain of music from an open window or doorway, the spell of the city gradually works its magic. The grace and ethereal beauty of the old town, its connection with an ancient, romantic past and lively present, instill in each of them a spontaneous excitement. They forget the closed tourist facilities, forget that they are simply postponing the final purpose of their journey, and surrender instead to a sense of wonder; and the illusion that these few days might somehow become cloaked in holiday raiment seems not so illusory after all.

And the experience of the old town stays with both of them into the night, even though their initial dissatisfaction with the place is justified: they do see a camping ground sign outside the town eventually, but when they follow it, they find that the ground is closed for the winter. It stays with them even when they decide to park the van outside the camping-ground's padlocked gates, then when Odette's halfway through cooking a meal, dogs begin to howl and bark from somewhere nearby: and the sound persists as they eat, drink with reflective cheer a bottle of champagne to see out the old year, clean up, and strip-wash themselves over a tub of heated water.

And then even when they resign themselves to the possibility of a kennels being close by and of the howling lasting all night, and later when Odette wakes in the early hours of the morning to cold air pressing like glass against her skin when she sits up to breastfeed a restless Jason, Odette still finds herself remembering the enchantment of the old town's rough thick walls and narrow, crooked windows, its glimpsed, elaborate courtyards and unexpected turrets, its castle battlements that seem to have grown quite naturally from the rocky outcrop on which they crouch.

She knows that the lives of the people in the town are probably hard and poor, and that beneath the facade of romance the town is probably grubby and cold and crowded and bitter; but she realises too that its people have something infinitely valuable nevertheless, something that gives their lives a richness it is impossible to measure, something the modern, smart, new world will forever be denied.

16

Miami Platja

In the morning, there is frost on the van's windows.

'Happy New Year.' Megan's voice, as she swings backwards down from her bunk above the cockpit, is brisk. 'What time did those bloody dogs stop barking?'

'Happy New Year to you, too.' Odette is changing Jason's nappy, still wrapped in her sleeping bag. 'I'm not sure, but Jason woke me about three and they were quiet then. Bit of a chilly night, wasn't it?'

'You're not kidding! Must be the elevation. As soon as we get down from this mountain range, it should be warmer.'

'I'm sorry – I never should have got you to come up here.'

'What? Oh, Odette, no, no! You don't think I'm blaming you, do you?' Megan is genuinely distraist. 'I didn't mean that at all – God, I'm the one who dragged you to a draughty twelfth-century castle in a snow-bound Massif Central, remember? I'm glad you're making some of the decisions – relieves my guilt about getting you to carry on with this thing. Anyway, you loved it, didn't you, the old town?'

Odette nods, her expression lightening.

'Well so did I. So it was worth it, wasn't it? Brrrr! I'll get the stove going in a minute, but first I'm busting to go to the loo. A big breakfast, do you think? We'll be on the road for quite a while, if we're to get to Valencia today. Don't think there's much to see between here and there, is there?'

Odette half-grimaces, half-smiles as Megan disappears into the cramped cubicle. So much for me making decisions, she thinks. But she won't get away with it that easily. Then it occurs to her that Megan's buoyant spirits, coupled with her reference to the castle, probably indicate that Luc has been in her thoughts, that she has been dreaming of him perhaps, and of a New Year plump with possibility. And immediately she thinks of Matt. And she frowns. What will the New Year bring for them?

Then Jason coos, and his hand waves against her cheek.

She looks down to his gummy grin and his father's eyes, and she smiles back. 'Can't be too bad as long as you're okay,' she says. She bends and kisses his face, his forehead and each cheek. 'I'm doing this for you as well as him, you know. If I can get Matt out of jail by the end of this month, and he can claim compensation, it'll all be worth it. It won't make up for the time he's missed with you, or whatever he's putting up with in that place, but it'll help.'

Then she picks him up and moves him to one side of the bed; she packs the bedding away before reassembling the cabin into a dinette.

*

They decide to take the N11 down as far as Mataro, then, noting the way that red road on the map disappears once it enters Barcelona, agree to use an *autopista* to bypass the Catalunyan capital.

The N11 runs parallel to the sea. Once they get past the grubby major tourist resorts which swerve the road slightly inland, the road flattens out and hugs the coast. They pass groves of a trim, plump fir trees, as fuzzy and neat as olive-coloured Afghan haircuts; white and green or red fishing boats coiled with dark straw rope; tumbledown turrets discreetly cosy against an occasional rocky outcrop; seagulls swooping and mewing over a Mediterranean as calm and gentle as a lake. The sand is very white and even, surely unnaturally so, and restaurants and bars, all closed, are built on the beach itself. If they pass through a town on the hour, they hear church bells dong strangely mournfully, although the chimes are probably meant to welcome in the New Year.

Near Mataro, they follow the signs to the *autopista*, but somehow miss it. With increasing unease, Megan manipulates the van through heavier and heavier traffic, across a landscape becoming either cramped with buildings which are ridiculously prickly with long spiky television antennae, like giant insects from some other planet, or flat and dusty and devoid of greenery.

On the outskirts of Badalona, they pass a gipsy camp whose poverty seems extraordinary: ragged children stand beside lean-tos built from scrap while adults tend fires or string washing between poles. It is a relief when just outside Barcelona, in eight-lane traffic, they see an *autopista* turn-off, and Megan swings the van toward it.

They emerge on the other side of Barcelona and manage to get onto a coast road again; but when they are confronted with a choice of toll-tunnels under a mountain range or a treacherous-looking strip of coast, Odette, remembering the road to Tossa de Mar, and fresh from the relief of the *autopista*, suggests firmly that they pay a toll again. Then, with growing confidence, she directs Megan to the N340, and it is just before midday when they decide to stop for lunch at a strip of beach called Miami Platja.

Odette volunteers to make up a picnic they can eat on the sand, and Megan, with a burst of goodwill partly generated by the relief of having successfully navigated Barcelona, offers to take Jason down to the water for a look around.

The sun is out, and warm, and it glints on a grey-blue sea. The sand on the beach is not white, as it had been further north: it is more the colour and texture of hard-packed brown sugar, and on it there are dredges of round, flat pebbles, left like waves by the sea. Megan puts Jason down, and he immediately crunches the sand in his fists then raises his hands to his mouth. She hastily picks him up again and brushes him down, then takes him down to the water to wash his hands.

The waves are calm, but icy: Jason squeals at their touch. She turns back then, guiltily, to see if Odette has heard, but there's no movement from the van. Instead, she sees across the road and towering against the skyline and over the tiny village at their base, the Montserrat mountains, huge, powerful, bare brown and jagged, wedged with clefts like a badly turned-out cake; and in front of them, on the beach side of the road, scrub which looks like a picture of South American rattlesnake country.

And then in the scrub, partly hidden from the road by it, she sees a camping ground sign.

Her first reaction is, I won't tell Odette and hope she doesn't notice it. But then she tilts her head sideways. They haven't done any clothes washing since France; and both of them badly need to wash their hair as well. This camping ground will probably be closed – but if it isn't, how likely is it that they will find another one open today? And the area is beautiful, in a stark, clean-lined, almost frightening sort of way. And Valencia is many hours' drive away.

Odette emerges from the van just then, with a plastic sheet and plates of food. Megan signals to her, indicating a smooth strip of sand. They eat sandwiches, of smoky cheese and tomato, and oranges, and Odette feeds Jason tinned vegetables in between her own mouthfuls. The sun is warm but the air cool.

Megan tells Odette about the camping ground.

*

The camping ground is very much open: surprisingly littered with caravans and cars. It is right on the beach, in ragged scrub, and has hot showers and a laundromat.

By the time they have cleaned themselves and their clothes and Jason has settled to sleep again – along with most of the campsite at their siesta apparently – it is almost three thirty.

'Do you mind watching Jason for a bit while he's having his nap?' Odette asks, seeing Megan pull out her notepad and pen and settle herself on the cushions in the dinette.

'Course not.' But Megan raises her eyebrows in question.

'Just thought I might go for a walk. Stretch my legs. It's so nice to be clean and fresh again – I feel as if I have to brush some cobwebs from my brain as well.'

'Good idea. I thought I might get out later for a stroll myself. But, Odette?'

Odette turns back from the cabin doorway. 'Yes?'

'I hope you're not…I mean, don't go and – well, *worry*, will you? About Dickson? Because I'm going to write the script for Alicante – thought I might start on it now, actually – and all you'll have to do is memorise it and rehearse it. Don't think about him, don't think about any of it, okay? I'll do the worrying. Nothing's going to go wrong.'

*

That's easy for her to say, Odette thinks, grimacing as she weaves towards the sea through the scanty brush: because she has, as Megan intuited, begun again on the long quiet drive to fret. It's not her baby… I mean, what if Dickson believes me? That Jason is his? What if he tries to snatch him, or something? Oh, God, but of course he won't. Why would he want to? What would he do with a baby? But what if he tries to *touch* me? I'll scream. I know I'll scream. Blow the whole thing. It's easy for Megan to say, don't worry about it.

But as she starts along a stretch of sand, she does, despite making no effort to, stop thinking about Dickson. The beach is very smooth and flat, and she watches wave after wave peel back like unfurling streamers in perfect tubes as far as she can see. If only they were bigger, she thinks, this would be a surfer's heaven. Then she comes across a shallow lagoon, left by the tide, like a miniature lake: it is blue, and white pebbles, all smooth and rounded, stud the edges of its bed.

Past the lagoon she comes across a washed-out building, as big as a bathhouse, with cutout turrets along its front wall. There is a rectangular doorway cut out on either side of this front wall, and the effect is of the facade of a castle. Odette approaches, intrigued; she peers cautiously into one of the doorways. Inside, it is quite dark: there appears to be no back doorway. As her eyes adjust, she makes out fishing tackle stacked on broken shelves, and then a grubby blanket on a box in a corner. And then she sees two other things: a syringe, thin and weak-looking, with a yellow ampule beside it; and a used condom, a slime of ooze dried glistening from it on the stone over which it is draped. And suddenly, in the darkest corner of the room, she senses movement.

She recoils, her hand turned to a fist at her mouth. She backs away, and stumbles on a tuft of spiky grass. She turns quickly, catching her balance, swinging her head hastily. She is filled with panic. Don't run, she thinks, don't run. She begins to move again, hastily, trying not to look back, or around, trying to slow her feet in their heavy boots, trying to reason herself out of such unreasonable fear. And, gradually, as no footsteps sound behind her, as the sea uncurls its locks of spreading foam closer to her hurrying feet with its hushing, gentle rhythm, she begins to calm. And comes back at length to the lagoon. She stops there, taking a deep breath; she looks cautiously over one shoulder, then the other. No one.

And then a flicker catches her eye. She starts, swivelling to the movement – from the lagoon, surely? Then sees it again: a shiver of movement just breaking the water, spreading ripples on what, now she looks at it from a different angle, is a grey and rather slimy surface. She watches, frozen, filled with dread. Sees another slight ripple, closer to her this time. Then sees what is causing it.

A large black and brown fish flicks its tail suddenly out of the water, only six feet away from the edge of the pond. A large black and brown fish, imprisoned in a scummy lagoon, circling. Waiting for the tide to return, to free it. Only now, looking at it closely, it seems to Odette that the lagoon is slightly stagnant, that it hasn't had a flush of clean water for quite a while.

She shudders, trying to shake off the thought of Dickson which has crept unwittingly back into her head, trying to shake off the unwanted, suddenly remembered, sensation of his tongue touching her skin, slipping over it, leaving a glistening slime.

17

Valencia

'I don't know why I was so frightened.' Odette sips the coffee laced with cognac Megan has made for her. Her face is regaining some if its colour, and losing its frozen grimness. At first Megan hadn't been able even to get her to speak. 'I mean, I don't know what I thought whoever it was was going to do to me. It was just the horrible *seediness* of it – the reduction of an act of love to such...' She doesn't finish.

'It reminded you of Dickson, didn't it?' Megan's voice is gentle.

'And then that fish.' Odette sips again, and shudders. 'I don't know whether I felt sorry for it, or wanted to kill it.'

Megan is silent for a moment. Then she says, 'I expect that's because you were associating it with a number of things. Dickson, Matt...us, stuck in the van, even?'

Odette shakes her head, holding the mug to her cheek. 'I don't know.'

'Look.' Megan puts out her hand and takes Odette's cold one. 'Talk about it – him, Dickson, if you want to. You probably need to. You've been bottling it up, submerging it – and you probably really need to deal with it somehow. I think...' She hesitates and then continues, 'I think it's terribly complex. I mean, it was rape, but not a rape you could report. Because you were compliant in it – because you agreed to it to stop Dickson arresting Matt for the dope bloody Dickson had planted in your house anyway – oh, the whole thing makes my blood boil!' She drops Odette's hand and reaches for the cognac bottle. 'Here, have another slug of this. Think I'll have one too.' She leans over to the sink for a glass.

'And the way he did it.' Odette's voice is low; she drinks from the mug automatically, staring at the table. 'He got me to take off my clothes and bend over the kitchen table, and he took me from behind, like a dog, as if I was a dog, or he was; and his fat belly slapped and sweated against me, and his hands, his bloody hands dug into my hips …and I was…' She has started to cry.

'Pregnant?'

Odette nods, and sobs, and hiccups out, 'He didn't know, but he wouldn't have cared anyway, but I was so worried I'd lose him, lose my little baby…'

'But you didn't.' Megan has taken Odette's hand again. 'You didn't. You have your beautiful little boy. And your beautiful little boy just might be Dickson's undoing. That great fat slob of a prick won't be able to resist the curiosity of seeing a child you will claim to be his – and curiosity killed the cat.'

Megan releases Odette's hand and picks up her glass again. She looks thoughtfully at Odette. 'You know what else besides having Matt out of jail will happen when we get this tape?'

Odette shakes her head.

'Your nightmares will stop, and your panic attacks. I'll bet you any-thing. It'd be worth it just for that if nothing else, don't you think?'

Odette closes her eyes, then looks back at Megan and nods.

'Right. Now let's get something on for dinner – and here, have an-other cognac. Help you sleep tonight. Cheap as chips here in Spain too – remind me to get some more tomorrow.' Because we're probably going to need it over the next few days, Megan adds mentally, but not verbally.

*

During the night it rains, and in the morning they wake to ragged, poi-sonous-looking clouds, green-yellow with heavy under-layers of grey. A cold wind blows in from the sea. They breakfast and shower again, and are on the road by ten o'clock. The Montserrat mountains tower to the west, bony-ribbed, their peaks lost under thick-foaming cloud.

The N340 hugs the Costa Daurada on the edge of the mountain range for most of the morning, but by eleven thirty they are out of Catalunya and the landscape flattens.

They stop for lunch at an ancient coastal town called Torre Blanca. On a deserted beach, Odette spreads out a picnic; behind them, shuttered, black-laced apartments – obviously only used in the tourist season – shore up what might be a ghost town, it is so quiet. The waves are cold, strong and grey, but clean; the sky is still piled with cloud.

At one o'clock, they head back to the highway, past rowboats up-ended in silent streets, as if the ocean has discarded them there; they see no one.

*

Megan approaches Valencia with caution. Odette has pointed out that the *autopista* on the map disappears into the city and only emerges on its southern side, as the N11 had in Barcelona; the N340 becomes a minor road as it nears Valencia – it changes colour on the map from red to yellow – so she suggests they stick to the N340 and try to find a campsite sign somewhere on the outskirts. But suddenly, before they realise it, they have entered the city and find themselves heading towards its centre.

Odette hastily pulls out the *Let's Go*. 'Don't panic,' she says, juggling the book over Jason's sleeping bulk. 'It says here that if we just keep on this road we'll go straight through to camping grounds at the southern edge – *and* it says the grounds are open all year!'

And really the traffic is not horrendous: it flows thickly but smoothly past a huge park planted over the diverted Turia riverbed. All along the park's edges are orange trees in – astonishingly, because it is midwinter – bright fruit, looking like half-decorated Christmas trees, or Carmen Miranda hats, because all the fruit within reach has been picked and the reddish globes bespangle only the treetops. The clouds have dissipated and the sun is bright.

Megan suddenly begins to change lanes; when the van is in the far right-hand one, she pulls off the road and up a side street. She swings into a car park under a row of skeleton trees edging towering, ugly apartment blocks.

Odette raises her eyebrows at Megan as the engine dies.

'I remembered something. You know how if you don't pay for a place in a camping ground up front, a lot of places keep your passports until you do? Well, we're a bit short of ready cash, and I don't really want to hand over our passports when we don't have visas. It suddenly occurred to me when I saw those blokes in military outfits back there – did you see them?'

Odette shakes her head. She had been looking at the orange trees. 'You're right, though.'

'I'm going to scout around and see if I can find a bank. It looked like a city centre back there: there's bound to be somewhere that'll accept MasterCard. Why don't you take Jason over to that park, stretch your legs, while I'm gone? I might try and ring Pete again, too, even if it is well past midnight in Australia. At least I should catch him! I won't be able to get through to Jerome at this time. I'll try him tonight.'

They part ways at a set of traffic lights, agreeing to meet back at the van at four thirty. Odette, conscious of Jason's overdue afternoon feed, crosses over to the park and begins to search for a semi-private bench in the sun on which to sit. She walks down a broad sandy avenue lined with orange trees, their dark greens and oranges so vivid in the sunlight they make her blink. How strange it is, she thinks absently, to have such green trees here, and such wintery ones in the streets.

Eventually, she comes to what seems to be a busy, roped-off playground – except that there are armed guards standing around its entrance: yet no one seems to be paying to enter it. There are timber bench seats on its perimeter. She hesitates, but Jason is becoming increasingly agitated; so she selects a bench as far away from the guards as possible, sits down, pulls a bottle of orange juice for herself from her shoulder bag, and settles Jason to her breast.

While Jason feeds, she looks at the playground curiously. It is enormous: it seems to be a series of broad, undulating slippery slides, with some sort of looped climbing jumble at the far end. There are intermittent white ropes pinned to the pebbled ground and then attached to rings on the sculpture: these often edge sometimes steep, sometimes shallow, steps, and children are using the ropes to pull themselves up to the slides. The steepest slide, a strip of black, is in the middle of the playground. The whole thing is made of painted, smooth concrete. There is a strange-looking glass-paned black building, shaped, she realises suddenly, like a tall hat, set apart from the main sculpture. She stares at the sculpture again: there are curious curves painted a pinky-orange at the base of one slide, presumably to cup sliders neatly after their fall. Then she sees what the curves are: the fingers of a giant human hand.

And suddenly the whole sculpture begins to take form. She sees that the black slide is in fact a belt, with a huge buckle in its centre; there is a boot, off, but bridged by a giant toe to the end of an enormous foot, at the base of a slide running down a black-clothed leg. She hears a loud squeal of delight, and watches a child shoot down the leg, bump over the toe, and slide in a graceful arc into the landing curve of the overturned boot.

Odette is fascinated. When Jason is finished, she takes him around to the entrance, nods to the indifferent guards, and begins slowly to circle the giant effigy.

It is of Gulliver; it has to be. The statue's clothes – a ruffled shirt, a black, tailed suit coat, a loose necktie (the climbing jumble), buckled boots, the Quaker-like hat – speak of the eighteenth century; the ropes pinned to the pebbles are surely meant to tie him down; the curved fingers, neat, black beard and closed eyes imply the figure is asleep or unconscious.

Why? she thinks. Why have a statue of Gulliver, an English literary figure, here in Valencia? It's marvellous, a superb idea, particularly because the sculpture seems so practically and imaginatively designed to be safe and fun for children: but why here? And why have armed guards to protect it?

There are no answers. But it seems to Odette, as she begins to slide Jason down some of the smaller slopes, holding him firmly under the arms, then at his obvious enjoyment of the movement, climbs to higher slides and goes down with him, that the guards look as useless in their job as the puny ropes do in their effort to tie down such a massive creature as this Gulliver. And as she climbs to higher and steeper slides, her heart pumping with a childish excitement, she thinks, how absurd such a creature as this would be! How absurd and unmanageable, how open to abuse of his power, such a giant would be!

Eventually, Odette straps Jason back to her chest. It is past four o'clock. She is standing back, taking one last look at the statue before heading back to the van, when she sees a door, tucked under Gulliver's shoulder. It opens and a mother and two children emerge.

Odette approaches the door curiously. It is slightly ajar. She opens it and goes in.

And sees that she has become the giant. Because inside there is the town of Valencia in miniature: she recognises this park, a church they passed on the way in, a square with tiny copies of statues she remembers. There are narrow streets which other giants are carefully picking their way through. Some of the roofs have been removed and she can, voyeuristically, peer into the frozen lives of the occupants.

And it is then that with a sudden shock she understands, for the first time, the recklessness power can induce. She stares around the room at all the tiny houses each of which, if she were a real giant and this a real town, she could if she wanted to crush with one stamp of her heel, all the streets she could wreck or repair at her will, all the lives she could invade or aid, at her whim.

And she recognises too that in the past she has always had a distaste for power, a discomfort with the responsibility it incurs, because she has had no faith in her own ability to make choices. But now, here, in Valencia, a day's travel from Alicante, she is filled with a sudden, all-pervading sense of the possibilities of her power, of her will. For the first time in her life, she acknowledges her *right* to change her world.

And she thinks, I'm going to make this work. Dickson might think he's a Gulliver, untouchable, but he's not. He's only a man. *I* could be Gulliver. Dickson could be like the Lilliputians, like those guards, in the face of my power – if only I believe I have it.

18

Alicante

'How did you go?'

Megan's sitting in the van studying the *Let's Go* when Odette's voice and the opening passenger door rouse her. 'Great!' Megan puts the book down. 'Found a bank pretty quickly. There seems to be a whole clustered financial area: very practical. And I got through to Pete. His wife wasn't too pleased to hear from me – can't blame her, it was one thirty their time – but he sounded cheerful enough. Apparently, Dickson is due back in Alicante tomorrow. But listen – listen to this bit of news! You know those two women who I couldn't get to lodge a statement against Dickson? The ones he'd tried the same shit on as you? Pete says they're coming around. He's told them about you coming over here with me, and they're getting close to making statements. To the police and us. Can you believe it, can you believe it?' She's jubilant, her brown eyes shining in their frame of blonde hair.

Odette is just about to take Jason into the cabin to change his nappy. She stops and stares at Megan. 'Michelle and Carol? You're joking,' she says slowly.

'No. No, I'm not. Well, Dickson's been out of the country for a month, and even though those women were shit-scared because of what happened to Matt when you wouldn't do what you were told a second time, I think they're beginning to see that the bastard might actually be able to be caught.'

Odette stares at Megan, then turns to go through to the cabin to find a clean nappy; her voice is a little muffled, but clear nevertheless when she replies. 'Well, they won't have to worry any more, after this week. Because Dickson is *going* to get caught. And even if he's not

151

charged, the whole case should be enough to make sure none of us, at least, get harassed ever again.'

Megan swings around in surprise to Odette, who in the dim light of the cabin continues, not looking up from unclipping Jason's britches, 'You know, Megan, when I agreed to come here with you, I really had no faith in any of it turning out. It was just that I felt so helpless sitting in that town back there, so *victimised*, that when you suggested this thing I went along with it.'

'I know. I realised that.' Megan's voice is hesitant; she swings her legs to sit sideways in the van seat, her forearms resting on her thighs.

'But now…it just occurred to me today. The whole thing that he did to me. *I should have stopped it*. Right at the beginning.' Odette pulls the damp nappy deftly out from under Jason and slips a clean one in its place. A ray of light slants through one of the windows across the baby. 'Right at the beginning, when he started following me, *watching* me…you know, he parked, on and off, in his police car outside my flat, and followed me if I went out – anywhere – for a *month* before he did anything more! A month. Why didn't I complain, phone the police department then – even tell *Matt?*'

She pauses: then she fastens the tape on Jason's nappy and begins to clip up his pants again. When she continues, her voice is breathy. 'Surely they'd have had to take notice?' She swings around, angrily. 'Why didn't I at least say something when he started appearing *in my house?* I told you about that, didn't I? He must have got a key cut, or had a master key. He'd just appear, in a doorway, when I was cooking, studying, watching television, in bed – he'd just appear, silently, and stand and watch me. Why didn't I say anything then? Because after that, when he came into the bathroom that night when I was in the bath, trapped, naked, the night he opened the door and stood there and dropped his pants from that fat, white, hairy belly and he…masturbated…'

Her voice drops with the last word; she looks up at Megan, her long black hair swinging back from her face, her eyes huge. 'I knew it was too late. He told me then what he would do to Matt if I said a word. And I knew what he was going to do to me next.'

Megan's watching Odette. Now she nods cautiously. 'Well, I had wondered…'

But Odette cuts her off. 'It was because he *froze* me. His police *uniform*… Do you realise how much power even a police uniform has? And his size, his confidence – his age. About as old as I remember my father being. When I was small, I was terrified of my father.' Her voice is suddenly harsh. 'Of his beltings, of the things he used to do to all of us and to Mum. The best thing that happened in my childhood was that he had a massive heart attack and died.'

Her voice cracks then; she ducks her head. But after a moment she props Jason up and begins to tidy his hood. When she looks back at Megan, her face is composed and her voice quiet. 'Do you understand? It was projected fear. Instinctive. Only I didn't see it at the time.'

Megan's brow is furrowed; she doesn't say anything.

Odette suddenly smiles. She takes a deep breath. 'It's okay. Don't look so worried. Because you see, now I think I can do something. Something. Maybe not anything unique, anything which will ultimately change much – but enough to satisfy me. And get Matt out of jail… I just, I guess, suddenly felt things from his – Dickson's – point of view. From the point of view of owning power. I'll tell you about it on the way to the campsite. We'd better get going, hadn't we, if we want to get settled before it's completely dark?'

Megan straightens slowly, still frowning. Then she shrug and grimaces. 'Um…yeah. Yeah, we had. It's not far, though. Looks easy enough to find. You don't want something to eat first?'

Odette shakes her head. 'I'll grab a couple of muesli bars for us to have on the way.'

'Okay.' Megan turns back to face the windscreen; she stares thoughtfully at the thick-shadowed, winter-branched street for a moment, then turns the key to warm the engine.

*

The campsite is at El Saler: open, enormous, but practically deserted, except for a thousand cats. Megan makes a spaghetti dish with tinned sardines and tomatoes and black olives and onion rings while Odette takes Jason off for a shower. Skinny, ragged cats mew around the van as the fish heats. When it's dark, apricot globe street lights stretch to the shower block like Jupiter's moons, or a string of giant luminous oranges; then all night long one of them flicks on and off rhythmically outside the van, and one little kitten meows pitifully, even after they feed it the scraps of their meal.

It is with relief that they dress in the shivery grey of dawn, pack up their beds in the eight a.m. sunrise, and prepare to leave for Alicante.

*

They drive past fields of wild white and yellow ground cover flowers with thick, dark green leaves, and hills either like grey elephants, bristly with furry shrubs, or like leopards, or adolescent male faces, tufty with spots and hair.

It is outside the city of Alicante that they see the signs for Muchav-ista camping ground, at San Juan de Alicante. They follow the signs to a little coastal village with a railway track running between it and a smooth, flat beach; they pull into a white-walled camping ground just before midday.

Megan stops the van in the space a gesticulating proprietor directs her to – in the 'Eeng-leesh' section, under gum trees. There are one or two other vans near them, but not nearly as many as in a French section even Odette recognises as such, because of the gutsy strains of an Edith Piaf tape issuing from one of the caravans, and a group of women set-ting a large table in a sort of makeshift courtyard with breadsticks and plates of sliced tomato and bottles of wine.

'Well, here we are.' Megan turns to Odette and they stare at each other for a long moment.

'So…what now?' Odette's voice is calm.

'Now, we orientate ourselves. Check out train times to and from

Alicante. Get a map and a feel for the town. Ring Jerome and see what he can tell us about Dickson's movements. Hopefully, I'll get through at this time of day – he must have gone out for dinner or something last night, 'cause I couldn't get through even the last time I tried. You were asleep when I got back. Then, depending on what Jerome says, finish writing the script. Plan our attack.'

Odette looks straight ahead, frowning, and nods. 'Okay. All right if I go to the toilet first?' She turns and watches Megan's intensity collapse into a lopsided grin.

*

'Hello, John.' Odette's voice is soft.

He swings abruptly, his neck first, then his body. His eyes are narrowed and his fists semi-raised.

'Didn't expect to see me here, did you?' Her heart is racing.

'Shit. Shit.' His eyes, bulbous in oysterish flesh, glitter sharply.

'I've come to find you.' Jason squirms a little, staring at him inquisitively. 'There's something I think you need to know.' She adjusts Jason's weight; the baby clings to her side, like a koala, looking too at Dickson. Dickson's eyes move suspiciously under his brows. 'He has your mouth, you know.'

'Who?' His voice is rude.

'My son.'

She can see his brain calculating dates: child how old? Young. How long since I fucked her? October? November? Hard to remember: there were others. Bit drunk at the time. Didn't see her when I tried it the second time: rang. She wasn't at the boyfriend's court case. Noticed that much. Dumped by him? Or too scared of me?

He stares at her, his eyes shiny and insolent as marbles. 'Dunno what you're talking about.'

She looks at him steadily. 'You owe me. You put Matt in jail. You planted half a kilo of heroin in the lining of his couch: double your original threat. I was surprised it wasn't more – all you could get your hands on from the police coffers, was it? You've wrecked my life. You've taken everything from me – and given me this in return.'

He stares at her, and suddenly his gaze is shifty. 'Why didn't you have a fucking abortion? And I didn't plant anything on anyone: your boyfriend was a dealer who got caught: now he's paying for it.'

'Paying for it? Paying for it? The only thing he's paying for is having a girlfriend you wanted to fuck.' Her voice is savage, but shaking. 'I know about you, John. I know all about the others. Four women are testifying against you in Australia right now.'

'So? So? I'm a Spanish citizen. They can't touch me.' His smile is contemptuous.

'Fuck.' Megan throws down her pen in disgust. 'Why can't I get this right? Every way I've tried it, I can't get him to confess. He's a policeman: he'll know every trick in the book. He'll be suspicious from the start. He'll be looking for tape recorders. And you're not an Oscar-candidate, Odette, I've got to tell you. These lines aren't making it.' She picks up her coffee mug and drains it.

Jason observes her from a nest of pillows against which he is propped beside Odette, on the other side of the table from Megan. He coos and waves his fists, then begins to gnaw on an index finger.

Odette chuckles to Jason, and strokes his mossy head before handing him a plastic ring. 'I think he's beginning to teethe. He's chewing on everything.' She turns back to Megan and picks up the script. 'But we can't predict what Dickson'll really say, anyway. Or exactly how either of us will react. Look, what do we know? That he likes the Santa Barbara castle. He's been going up there every day for the last few days, walking up to it instead of using the lift. Probably feels justified then in going out to restaurants and gorging himself, then sleeping all afternoon. With some poor unlucky prostitute, probably. So. This is the best place to tackle him, we've agreed. If luck's on our side and he keeps to that routine. And what I most want him to confess is his name and the fact that he planted dope on Matt. The rest, I'll bring up, but it's not as important. So let's look at the three scripts you've written and try to combine them to focus on that, no matter what happens.'

My God, Megan thinks: look at her. She's changed. Something on this trip has changed her. All the way, she's been so frightened of arriving here – and now we've made it, where is her fear? She's strong. She's become strong.

*

They wake to rain. The morning is cold and grey, a wind spattering drops like plastic beads on the van roof. Odette makes breakfast quietly and Megan is silently tense as well. They dress carefully. Megan wears her usual jeans, pullover and anorak, but ties a black scarf over her blonde hair and puts on pair of round, cheap sunglasses she found the evening before in a convenience store where they'd bought bread, milk, a surprisingly fresh chicken, complete with head and claws as the chickens had been in France.

Odette shakes out a long velvet skirt, a low-cut jumper, and her long hooded coat. The portable tape recorder she hooks up carefully from an inside pocket of the coat. She dresses Jason in maroon and yellow, colours which suit him, takes an umbrella from the van closet and slings a nappy bag over her shoulder.

They follow directions to the train station that Megan secures from the French sector of the camping ground. By ten o'clock, they are on their way to Alicante.

*

The train is modern, electric. Odette sits on the sea side with Jason on her lap. For a while, the train line runs parallel to the brown, rainswept beach, then veers inland, to enter smoggy townships. Odette tenses as they approach Alicante, and takes a deep breath when Megan nudges her and begins to adjust her coat and gather up her carry bag. They disembark into a shelter on the edge of the beach at the foot of the Santa Barbara cliff.

157

Both Megan and Odette stare up in awe at the mountain. Its base is solid rock, the colour of the inside of a Violet Crumble bar, and at its summit towers the Santa Barbara castle, carved from the rock itself. The old town of Alicante huddles defensively under and to the left of the castle, while new, ugly, Lego constructions swarm like a mechanical army around both the old town and the rest of the mountain base. Sand laps at the foot of the rock, and what looks to be a tourist beach, edged with a red-tiled pavement, spreads in its shadow. The rain is easing.

It is eleven o'clock.

'Right.' Megan lowers her gaze from the mountain to Odette. Let's take the lift, shall we? Then we can wait at the top for him. If he sticks to schedule, he should arrive in about half an hour.'

They follow the arrows and symbols to the castle elevator, which apparently shoots in a vertical tunnel right through the centre of the mountain. They wait in line to buy tickets with Japanese and American tourists, a well as some Spaniards. Eventually, the lift gates part and a uniformed, stiff-faced lift operator allows them in. The lift becomes crowded. He is just about to close the gates again when he pauses; Megan sees, around the bulky shoulder of an anoraked American, a last passenger hastily buying a ticket. The lift operator waits respectfully. The passenger speaks to the operator briefly in Spanish as he shuffles his bulk against the bodies behind him; then he turns his head to throw a '*Perdone*' over his shoulder.

And both Megan and Odette see his face.

Dickson.

19

Dickson

Odette's face is drained of colour. Megan sees that the knuckles of Odette's hands, clutched around Jason in his sling, are white also. Her eyes, huge, flicker. Megan swallows her own alarm and takes a deep breath. She nods just perceptibly as Odette turns to her. The elevator whines breathlessly up through the centre of the mountain.

Odette stares at the back of Dickson's neck, vividly real between the hooded heads of two tourists. The flesh is cross-hatched and red, the hairs on it greying. There is a round bald patch on the back of his head. She can see the tip of his nose in profile: fleshy, large-pored; and an eyebrow bristling below dull wisps of grey fringe. He turns his head, and she sees the folds of fattened skin draping back from his weak chin, and the film over an eye: bluish, transparent as a fish's. She swallows, staring at him. A fish, yes, that is how she remembers him: oyster-eyed and cold-fingered, his belly, slung from his ribs to his loins, slapping against her back. His penis, stiff, ramming, like serrated scales because she was so tense...

Megan nudges her. The lift has stopped. She can't take her eyes from him: she moves mechanically into a dim castle chamber she barely notices. They follow the other tourists and Dickson's black-coated bulk past gift shops and display rooms: some of the group deviate into these, but Dickson continues with a small crowd along a broad corridor: towards ascending steps, at the top of which Megan glimpses grey daylight. The fortress roof. Megan puts a hand on Odette's arm and draws her back from her seemingly automatic following of Dickson: draws her instead into the cold shadow of the stairwell.

'Look.' Megan's voice is urgent. 'God knows why he's come up early, and in the lift – it might be because of the rain, but it might also be because he's meeting someone. If it's still raining or even too overcast, I don't know how much the video camera will pick up, but I think we'll have to risk it anyway. He hasn't noticed us: we mightn't have the advantage of surprise another time. Are you okay? Are you going to be able to go through with it?'

Odette's face is frozen, but she nods. 'Now or never.' Her voice is a whisper.

Megan stares at her for a moment, then nods decisively. 'Wait here a moment.' She dumps her carry bag beside Odette, tucks loose strands of blonde hair under her scarf, pulls up her anorak hood, and slips up the steps.

After a few minutes, she returns, breathlessly, to bend and rummage in the bag. 'Okay. This luck can't hold. It's the perfect spot – he's gone to the far end: down into some sort of observation post, from the look. Circular, chest-high walls. Could be admiring the sea view – or watching for someone coming up by road. The angle of the lookout must give a good view of both. We're going to have to act quickly. There's a few other people near him, but he might, just might, stay longer than the others. If he's waiting for someone. Enough other people around for me not to be too conspicuous, as well, if I'm careful.'

She straightens, fiddling with the camera. 'I'll slip along the parapet to the right. I can set up the camera in a roofed alcove there. Some sort of entrance to a dungeon, I think. It should keep the rain off if it gets heavier, and give me some cover as well. Plus, the wind is coming from the sea, so from that angle your umbrellas shouldn't block my vision if you need to keep them up. Still spitting a bit. Anyone noticing me *might* think I'm videoing the panorama with the parapets and lookout post in the foreground – pretty silly in this weather, but tourists *do* do silly things sometimes.'

She pauses, unzipping her anorak and tucking the camera inside it; when Odette doesn't reply she glances up sharply. 'You sure you're all right?'

Odette takes a deep breath, then nods again. 'Yes. How long should I wait?'

'Only a couple of minutes: we mightn't have much time. Try to get him to turn in profile to me if you can. Now, don't forget to turn on the tape recorder before you follow. All right?'

'Yes.' Odette's mouth is grim and her eyes large.

'Good luck, then. Follow me to the top of the stairs, then wait till I'm ready.' Megan grimaces quickly, hesitates, then squeezes Odette's wrist. She leads the way up the steps, checks the roof, then moves out into the fine rain.

Odette fumbles with her umbrella. She watches Megan position herself, inconspicuously, professionally. 'All right, little one,' she says under her breath. 'All right. I did that for your father. Now I can do this. I can do anything, can't I? As long as I keep my head.' She takes a deep breath and adjusts Jason's weight and the nappy bag. She switches on the recorder, steadies her hand on the umbrella handle, and steps onto the wet stones.

She looks around cautiously. It takes her only a couple of seconds to find the lookout post, and to see that Dickson is still in it, with his back to her, his umbrella angled to the sea against the rain. There is one other person near him. She moves slowly toward them, checking Megan in her peripheral vision. She pauses, pretending to admire the view from a parapet, until Dickson's neighbour straightens from leaning on the thick wall, and turns. Then she advances as unhurriedly as she can.

'John Dickson.'

He turns sharply, swinging his whole body around. Odette treads slowly toward him, her umbrella high and steady. They stare at each other – oddly, Megan notices from her alcove as she adjusts the camera focus, similar in shape: Dickson with his slung fat belly and Odette with Jason slung below her breasts to her hips, both of them with high-tilted umbrellas. Then she zooms her lens in on Dickson's face: and sees that he doesn't recognise Odette.

Odette sees that too: and immediately all her rehearsed lines dissolve. But he must, he must remember me, she thinks; he couldn't forget, just *forget*.

'I…you…' she stutters; then she says, quite simply, staring at him, 'I came because Matthew is in jail. And because I've had a baby.'

Dickson stares back at her and she watches recognition relax the pouches under his cheeks into dewlaps, then sees him stiffen and his eyes flicker. And at that moment she realises he will turn his head, and see Megan, and that it will all be for nothing… And she lets her umbrella suddenly slip. He fumbles automatically to catch it. Then, before he can right himself properly, Odette has the umbrella collapsed and its sharp steel point suddenly rammed clumsily into his belly. He recoils, with a yelp, dropping his own umbrella and grabbing at hers to deflect it.

He tries to wrestle it from her, but she grips it with both hands, her heart pounding; and she sputters, 'You remember. You planted half a kilo of heroin in the lining of Matt's lounge. He's got six months for that. He's never dealt in his life. Not in heroin, not even in marijuana. He's tried them, tried most drugs – but he was never a junkie and he never dealt. God knows what he'll be like, though, when he gets out of that place!' Her voice has risen steadily: she is vaguely astonished at her own fluency and daring: but then even as the last phrase fades from her lips, her heart falters – oh, she thinks, I shouldn't have said that, not yet, not yet…

But he is still struggling with her umbrella, and she has no time to think: all she has is a reflex action, learned as a child in similar possession-wrestles with her siblings: she releases the umbrella suddenly, and Dickson falls backwards against the stone wall. She snatches up his umbrella before he can recover. She flips it to a point and stares at him across its length, panting. A fresh gust of rain rushes a shudder along her neck; Jason, awoken, begins to whimper.

'Odette.' He doesn't take his eyes from her, but cautiously straightens, her umbrella gripped firmly. 'And Matthew. Yes, I remember you.'

'*Remember me? Remember me?* What, I don't look the same when you're not following me, when I'm following you? Look different, do I, now I'm not your *prey* any more?'

She can see his quick darting look behind her, to check on who she might be with, or who's noticed the ruckus, but she semi-lunges at him again and his attention reverts to her. The rain falls softly on both of them as they pause, frozen, their umbrellas like absurd swords.

'What do you want?' Dickson says, slowly.

'What do I want? I want you to come back to Australia, to admit that you planted that heroin on Matt, and admit you blackmailed me and God knows how many others. That's what I *want*. But that's not going to happen, is it? You've escaped everything so neatly, haven't you?' Her voice is bitter. 'So I've come here to ask you only to sign a statement saying that you set Matt up. Is that so very much to ask? Forget about the blackmail, forget about your rape of me, if you haven't already! Forget about this baby.' She flicks her head at whimpering Jason, but doesn't take her eyes from Dickson.

He stares at her, then drops his gaze to Jason's yellow hood. 'What does your baby have to do with it?'

'Will you sign a statement, or not?'

He is standing fully upright: he has recovered. He could push her out of his way with one thrust – but he doesn't. He looks at Odette, at the beads of rain slicking her black hair to her forehead, at her eyes huge with anger and adrenalin – and back at the yellow hood of the baby crying into her breast. 'I said, what does your baby have to do with it?' he says softly.

'What do you think? *You* calculate dates!' She spits the words out.

He stares at her; his expression is strange. 'You would have had an abortion.' His voice is slow.

'In Rockhampton? Or Biloela perhaps? It's against the law, in case you've forgotten!'

'It could just as easily be your boyfriend's.'

'Do you think I could let *anyone* touch me, after what you did to me?'

Jason has begun to cry in earnest, but for the first time in his life, Odette ignores him. She stares at Dickson. 'I need him, I need Matt.

He thinks Jason is his… God knows, his life is going to be hard enough as it is…'

There is a long silence.

Then, 'Six months is not so bad,' he says, abruptly. 'If you hadn't been a good little girl to start with, he might have been caught with a kilo. Get at least a year for that.'

They stare at each other again – he at her black damp hair and wide eyes and fierce stance – she at his fish-eyes and thin hair in wet streaks across pale scalp, and oily flesh and sagging skin… And she thinks, *he knows that I'm taping him*.

And then, strangely, unexpectedly, despite what she knows of him, despite her utter humiliation by him, despite her brimming hatred of him, she feels her heart twist in a strange sudden spasm of pity. She slowly lowers her umbrella, and steps back, out of his path. 'Tell me –'

He is past her, striding towards a crowd of tourists who seem to have gathered to watch them from a distance; but he turns at her quieter voice, a voice almost gentle.

'– are you happy here? Are you happy, living in this raped country without ever lifting a finger again? Happy with your memories?'

But he says nothing, only looks at her, and at Jason, for a moment; then he walks quickly away, across the uneven stones, toward the dark shelter of the castle corridors.

*

'I, I don't know what was happening at the end there. I…was beginning to lose it. I was starting to feel *sorry* for the bastard – can you believe that? He looked so old and ugly – and do you know, I think he actually *hoped* Jason was his? How could someone even begin to think like that? To hope for a child of what was effectively rape? Oh God, my God, it's so pathetic, isn't it? So bloody, bloody *pathetic*.' Odette's voice cracks on the last word, and she sniffs loudly, throwing back her head and pushing her hands up over her eyes. When she takes her hands away, her eyelashes are damp.

'There's nothing to be sorry about.' They're sitting at the van table and the rain is drumming steadily on the roof; Megan reaches across and rubs Odette's cold fingers. 'It was right, everything's all right. It's enough. I really think it's enough. The tape's a little unclear, but I had your faces in close-up the entire time, so you can practically lip-read what you say anyway. You did really well, Odette. Magnificently. I'll get it all sent straight off to Pete this afternoon, express. Once it hits the papers, they'll have to release Matthew – and compensate him. I'm sure of it.'

'Oh, I don't know, I don't know. He didn't actually admit...'

'Yes he did. By not denying what you said, and by just that last thing. *"If you hadn't been a good little girl to start with, he might have been caught with a kilo. Get at least a year for that."* It's enough. It's an admission. Maybe not enough to get Dickson back for a trial, but surely enough to prove he blackmailed you. It's over now, all over. Here – drink up.' She pours cognac into the glasses she's already set out on the table.

Odette swallows dutifully. Megan watches her, and sees her face regain its steadiness, and a faint pink stain her cheeks. She allows herself then her own quick kick of excitement, and refills both their glasses.

They are silent for a moment.

Odette swirls the amber liquor around her tumbler, then says abruptly, 'It was worthless, wasn't it? I mean, all the things he did, and he winds up here, in this ruined country. I called it a raped country – did you hear that on the tape? It just occurred to me, right then: that Spain's been raped for the tourist dollar, wrecked, ugly, and I thought it was going to be so beautiful – by people like Dickson, probably, who only think about their own needs and wants. But what's he got here? No friends, no life, only foreign relations whose language he can barely speak. Lots of money, but nothing really worthwhile to spend it on.' She sips the cognac again, and shudders. 'He'll be like Christopher Skase, won't he? Never be able to return to Australia, not once there's a proper investigation. Unless he's willing to go to prison.'

The rain gusts suddenly on the roof and windows and drops of water fall on the table from the roof vent.

Megan stands on her seat to tighten the catch. 'Well, I can't see him choosing that option, can you?'

Odette doesn't answer; instead she huddles inside her coat and watches Megan's fiddling meditatively. Then she says slowly, 'Why did he do those things to me and those other girls, do you think? For love? Do you think he was really looking for love? Love no one would give him? But you can't just *steal* love. It'd be like trying to steal…a sandcastle, wouldn't it? Useless. You'd just destroy it for everyone.' Her voice is quiet and reflective; she looks up at Megan with a frown.

But Megan unexpectedly laughs. 'Well, that depends, doesn't it? What if you stole it by fencing it off? Staking it out as yours? Actually *preserving* it from destruction!' She flops back onto her seat. 'Oh, look, Odette, don't be under any illusions about Dickson! He did what he did for power. Taking what you would never have given freely. Dominating you, making you submit. Making himself feel strong, superior, clever. Well now, he is going to have to submit. Now he's going to pay. Even if it's only with his lack of freedom to ever leave this country.'

Megan's eyes glitter even in the subdued light in the van cabin: glitter, Odette sees, with excitement and victory. 'Do you think if human relationships meant anything to him, he would have done what he did? Don't waste your pity on him. He's got his villa by the sea, his lunches in restaurants, even if they're by himself, his cheap booze and siestas. He's not responsible to anyone or for anyone, and you can be sure he likes it that way!'

Odette lowers her eyes to the dinette table: its plastic veneer is scratched and the black plastic strip around it is unsticking. She frowns again. 'Oh, yes, yes, I know. It's just – when he thought just for a minute that Jason might be his… I wonder why he's like that, what happened in his past to make him so…'

'For God's sake, Odette, don't pull Christian forgiveness on me, please!'

Odette looks up sharply, shaking her head. 'No. No, I can't forgive him for what he did to me. I'm just trying to understand it, that's all.

166

How he could think any of it could be worth anything, in the end. What made him do it – caused the need, in the first place?

'Easy. Lust, greed, pride…'

'Insecurity?'

'Odette!'

'All right, all right. Sorry.' She smiles suddenly then, her face relaxing and lit up and suddenly youthful again, as Megan hasn't seen it for days. 'I just can't believe it's over!'

Megan stares at her, then collapses back suddenly with a crow, her head hitting the window. 'You said it, girl!'

'It was so incredibly sudden! I mean, there he was, in the lift with us. If he'd recognised us…'

Megan rubs her head, smiling. She sits forward again with her eyes alight. 'I know! It could have blown the whole thing.'

'Yeah.' Odette has her elbows resting on the table. 'And then – oh, it was so…well, bizarre! The umbrellas…'

And Megan begins to laugh again. Her eyes shine and she looks joyous. 'God, I hope I caught all that! What was all that about?'

'Oh, well…' Odette shrugs and half-smiles. 'If…if he'd turned his head, he'd have seen you.'

'Yeah? But of course.' Megan's face is uplifted in the candlelight. 'Hey, kiddo – that was pretty smart.'

'Thanks.' Odette feels her cheeks reddening. 'It was so incredible. The whole thing. I couldn't believe it was happening… Anyway. It's over. Strange. I've almost got, like, a let-down feeling. But…do you know, I think – I really believe – I'm not afraid of him any more. I don't think –' She throws a quick glance at Megan. '– you quite knew how I've felt, living in this van and everything.'

Megan purses her lips, then shrugs. 'Perhaps not. We're very different women, you and I.'

'Yes.' Odette's mouth twists suddenly. 'It would never have happened to you, would it? Dickson wouldn't have dared try it on you.'

Megan looks at her silently. Then gives a swift grin. 'But you're the one who nailed him, Odette! You!' Megan reaches out and tightens her fingers around Odette's again impulsively. 'Oh, look, this is a major cause for celebration! Forget about analysing the prick. Let's get dolled up – let's go out to a restaurant – let's eat paella and drink sangria and see some Spanish dancing.'

'But – what about Jason? And what if we run into… I don't know.'

'What about Jason? He can come with us. You never know, if he's awake half the night, he might sleep through the other half. Come on, Odette! The chances of running into Dickson are a thousand to one. Okay?'

Odette lifts her glass and looks at Megan through it. Then she swallows the cognac, gasps and smiles. 'Okay.'

20

Flight

They sleep late. The rain is quite gone and white-gold sunlight plays through the leaves of the gum tree beside the van, and through the pattern in the lace curtains.

Odette wakes with a start, checks immediately that Jason is still breathing – then relaxes back onto her pillow. We had fun, she thinks. What a night!

They had caught the train back into Alicante, and found a quiet bar in the old city at seven thirty. They had drunk with ice in tall tumblers sweet, richly golden Liquor 43, and eaten various tapas: stuffed mushroom heads strongly flavoured with garlic, finely sliced smoked ham, a platter of fried squid, a dish of fragrant, spiced green beans. Despite the noise and colour of the bar, by nine o'clock Jason was asleep in his sling, and the heavy-breasted, bright-eyed wife of the proprietor, streaming rapid and musical Spanish and clearly comprehensible body language, convinced Odette to relinquish him to a brightly quilted bench in an alcove behind the bar.

And thus Odette and Megan had eaten their main meal in peace: a crisp, lemony green salad, a frying pan of paella, thick slices of hard-crusted bread, and a pitcher of sangria which the young, dreamy-eyed barman had doused liberally with liqueurs he indicated Odette to choose from his shelves. Then guitarists had begun to strum, and the barman had sung, after much encouragement, deep-throated, tragic arias, his gaze directed again and again to Odette. And oh, Odette had thought, if I did not have a baby! Or Matthew trusting me!

But I do, she thinks now, the morning after, eyeing the fringed wings of Jason's sleeping eyelids; and I would not give my baby up for the world.

Not for the world.

As for Matthew…she sighs. She thinks of his glossy black curls, the jewel-blue flash of his eyes, the glitter of his diamond earring. There are going to have to be some changes, she thinks. When he's released. I need his support, now. Jason and I both do. I'm going to have to clip his wings, she thinks, a little sadly. He's going to have to live with us and help support us. Wild ways and babies don't go together. That's the reality. That's his…price.

She sighs again, noticing that her breath still vaporises slightly in the morning air. It's time to go home, she thinks. There's no reason to stay any longer. It's time to go back to sunny Queensland, to sun-soaked hot decks and shady mulberry trees and beaded pitchers of iced water. To my mother, with all her presents for Jason and me, and her reproaches about Jason's deprivation of his first Christmas. Her acid comments about Matthew. And later, her horror when it all comes out in the papers, when she hears about what really happened to her second daughter.

She sighs again. She thinks, will it all be worth it? Seeing justice done? Going through all of it, for justice? And forcing Matthew to face up to what I've done for him?

She stares at the patterns of sunlit lace playing across her sleeping bag, and at her breath dissipating gently in the light. And suddenly, irrelevantly, she thinks, well, if nothing else, I know one thing: I want to come back to this country, ruined and plundered as it is; I want to come back when it's warmer, to its velvety-voiced barmen and its wealth of history; and I want to play on its beaches with Jason and swim in its waters – all the things I can enjoy because I am young and healthy and *good!*

That's all I know.

*

Megan takes Odette to the El Altet airport on the outskirts of Alicante. From there, she can travel to Barcelona, to catch a connecting flight to Australia.

'Are you sure you don't want me to navigate you back up to France?' Odette's frowning, standing uncertainly in the air-conditioned lounge with her luggage around her feet.

'Oh, look, I think I'll just get onto the *autopista* after this and shoot the hell out of here.' Megan stoops to tie a luggage ticket onto a suitcase handle. 'I mean, it's really not that far, compared to the huge distances we travel to get around Queensland. I'll stop in Valencia again, then somewhere near the border tomorrow night, then head back up to Paris...'

'But I thought Luc was going to come down to spend a few days with you?'

Megan shrugs, but her pink cheeks betray her as she straightens. 'Oh, well, I'd rather just get the van back to Paris as fast as possible. Besides, I think we've run out of time: it's Thursday – he has to go back to work on Monday...cutting it a bit fine.' She threads string through another luggage tag. 'But he offered to put me up for a few days in his place in Paris before I fly home. Mind you, he's probably hoping I won't take him up on that. When you get to my age...'

'Which is, by the way?'

Megan smiles, broadly, at that. 'My, haven't you become more assertive! Here, give me Jason for a moment and you can tidy up the rest of your stuff: best to have tags on everything. Spain is notoriously badly organised, you know...'

But Odette has her head on one side, and eyes firmly on Megan's.

'All right – thirty, if you must know. Now give me Jason. Thank you. So, as I was saying, when you get to my age, you get a little cynical about things.'

'A little?'

'Oh, all right, very cynical – and stop getting so cheeky!'

Odette smiles then, straightening Jason's long pants, the legs of which have slipped up in the exchange of slings from her shoulders to Megan's. 'I don't think Luc would let you down. I thought he was lovely.'

'Which is precisely what I'm saying, and precisely why I do think he'll let me down. Lovely people invariably have their unlovely side…' Megan too is fussing with Jason's clothes.

'And prickly people like you invariably have their soft hearts! But Megan?'

Megan bites off her quick retort, and gingerly runs her hands over the bulk of the baby strapped to her torso; she raises an eyebrow silently at Odette.

'I – hope it does work out. Really. Will you contact me, let me know, when you get back? I mean, I know it's really none of my business, but –'

'Listen, kiddo, you certainly haven't seen the last of me: I'm going to be conducting the television interviews, writing the follow-up articles…'

'I know. But will you let me know how things turn out for you?'

Megan considers. 'Depends. If good, okay. If not, probably not. Sorry.'

The airport intercom suddenly gongs, and a stream of Spanish ensues. They both look up at the flashing electronic notice board.

'That's my flight call.'

'Better get your bags checked in, then. Here, give me those stickers: I'll put them on your hand luggage.'

Odette hesitates, then hands over the slips of paper. 'All right. Thanks. I won't be a minute.' She picks up her cases and disappears behind a group of Spaniards chattering excitedly around a young couple who have obviously just returned from somewhere.

Megan lowers herself awkwardly into a plastic chair at the end of an aisle. 'So this is what it feels like to be heavily pregnant,' she mutters to Jason.

He looks up at her solemnly.

She pulls Odette's bags to her feet and begins plastering stickers. 'Not that you'll ever have to worry about that,' she adds.

He watches her face with a slightly puzzled expression.

And then, before she is really aware of what she is doing, she straightens from the luggage, brushes a hand over his soft fine hair, and drops a kiss onto it. 'You know, you're really a very sweet baby. Except that you don't sleep enough. Make me almost clucky.' She looks down at his face again, and smiles. 'Wouldn't my father love to hear me say that.'

Jason stares at her, then suddenly smiles wetly back – and Megan sees a thin white rim in the middle of his bottom gum.

'But – oh my God, it's a tooth! Your first tooth!' She feels absurdly excited – then pulls herself up, glancing around hurriedly.

One of the Spaniards has turned to look at her.

'Does your mother know?' she asks more conspiratorially, fiddling with the luggage stickers. 'Bet she doesn't… Here she comes. Think I should tell her?'

Jason waves his hands, and makes a little cooing sound; Megan finishes the last sticker and sits up as Odette approaches.

'Thanks, Megan. I'll take him now, if you like. I can board in a minute, apparently.'

'Oh. Oh, all right then. Here you go.' Megan stands clumsily and wrestles out of the sling. 'Must be terrible for your back, this thing.'

'You get used to it. Although he is getting a bit too heavy for it. Be good to be able to put him in a pram again. Thanks.'

They walk in awkward silence to the boarding gate. Megan loads the hand luggage onto Odette's shoulders.

'Well, I – hope everything goes well with Luc.'

'Yeah, well, so do I, but if it doesn't…*tant pis*. Too bad,' she adds hurriedly: subconsciously, she realises, she is already slipping into French. 'I'll ring you when I get back, but expect a call from Pete before then.' She makes her voice brisk and professional again. 'I've given him your mother's address and number. Best if you don't let too many people know that's where you're staying. Just a precaution. Okay? Well, have a good flight. I'll get going.' She stands awkwardly.

Odette reaches out for her hand, and leans over Jason's bulk to kiss Megan's cheek. 'Thank you. Thank you for everything.' Her skin is cool and smooth and her long black hair brushes Megan's arm.

'That's fine. Thank you. It's been tremendously difficult, I know, but you were great. Really.' Absurdly, Megan's vision is blurred. She blinks quickly, and drops her head to plant a peck on Jason's cheek. 'Oh, I almost forgot. Check out Jason's mouth when you get the chance. Who says I don't know anything about babies? Better go. Bye.' She raises a hand, grins unsteadily and turns away.

Odette watches Megan's brisk stride and neat blonde head until Jason coos and touches her arm with a fist; only then does she look down at him, and gently lift his mouth to her line of vision.

21

Return

So now I'm alone, Megan thinks. She sits in the camper van, waiting for the engine to warm and for the heating to kick in. The almost fluorescent sunshine of the morning has dulled; grey-bellied clouds squat heavily on the horizon. Her fingertips are cold. 'And it's going to rain again,' she mutters aloud. There's a roar, a dull rumble, above the throb of the warming diesel, and she cranes through the windscreen at the sky. Thunder? Or Odette's plane? Perhaps neither.

I should really head straight back to Australia too, she thinks. Forget about Luc. Keep the memory intact. But she grimaces. Far too wise a decision for me! she thinks. Can't do it.

She frowns out at the clouds and at the mountains to the west, which tower like huge chunks of quartz over an otherwise flat landscape soft with green fuzzy trees. There are forces of nature, she thinks, much more powerful than any wisdom my brain concocts.

*

On her way back to the Muchavista campsite, the rain hits. Grey swaths of droplets pummel the van and Megan drives edgily with the lights on, conscious of the dredges of her hangover from the restaurant the night before. She pulls with relief into the camping ground, and parks under her familiar gum tree with a shudder from both the van and her anoraked shoulders. She switches off the engine and stumbles quickly out to open the little sealed partition in the side of the van which protects the gas regulator: she turns the wheel on with rain gusting against her legs. She slams back into the driver's seat, and from there through the grey-curtained partition into the van cabin, with relief.

The storm settles in then. She pulls all the velvet curtains across the lace ones, so the cabin is in almost darkness: rain slashes against the windows, and wet wind rocks and tumbles savagely about the thin metal walls. She pulls off her wet coat and hangs it from a hook between the cockpit and the cabin, before dragging a jumper over her head. Then she pulls out the gas heater and gets it going, makes herself coffee, and huddles in what was sometimes a dining room, sometimes a bedroom, but which is now only a cabin with foam cushion benches on either side.

And feels suddenly and completely how alone she is.

*

But the despondency doesn't last long. When the storm begins to ease, she pulls on her damp anorak and ducks out into the thin shower of still falling water, across to a pay phone in a dilapidated and deserted games room near the camping ground office. She dials the Parisian number Luc gave her.

'Allô, oui?'

'Allô, Luc?'

'Oui. Qui est-ce?'

'It's Megan.'

'Megan! Where are you?' Is it her imagination, or has his voice gentled and quickened in the switch to English?

'I'm still in Alicante, but Odette's gone back to Australia. At least, she's on her way.'

'Ah! So you have your story?'

'Oh yes, yes I think so. Should break in Australian papers soon, if all goes well. I – still shouldn't really talk about it until then.'

'Yes. I understand.'

'Look – I haven't got heaps of coins. I – just wondered whether you still wanted to see me again, when I bring the van back to Paris.' Her heart has begun to throb; she leans against the plastered wall beside the pay phone and stares absently at the vacant games room, with its worn pool tables and silent pinball machines, and at the fine rain slipping silently down the plate glass of the windows.

'So – you don't want me to join you in Spain?'

Megan bites her lip. 'Well, it's going to take me a couple of days to get the van back – I'm supposed to hand it over on Sunday, so I want to be back by Saturday at least: clean it up and everything. I could extend the lease – but...'

'Megan!' His voice is shocked. 'You cannot drive so far in this time... It must be – oh, fifteen hundred kilometres! *Ce n'est pas possible!*'

'Well, I know, but – I'm used to driving long distances. With my job. In Australia, where the roads are not nearly as good as they are here. Really. If I leave this afternoon, I can break the trip into three blocks. Be back Saturday night.'

There is a short silence, then, 'Well, if you really think you can do it. I have only some days before I go back to work, so perhaps it is best this way.'

She feels the familiar irritation rising against him then, despite its irrationality and her registering the doubt in his voice. Why, oh why, she thinks, couldn't you say, No! That's absurd! That's far too far to drive on your own, and such a waste of time we could spend together! No, I'll fly down to Alicante tomorrow and drive back with you! But then she sighs. Because I come across as such a strong, independent woman...

'You must come here, to my apartment,' he is saying. 'It's a bit cold in Paris at the moment – we've had more snow – but it is beautiful, just the same. You have never seen it, I think, in winter?'

'No. Only spring and summer. A little of autumn. Are you sure?'

'Yes. Yes, of course. You still have the address?'

'Yes – it's here with your phone number.' She takes another deep breath.

But he's saying, 'Even so, you won't want to drive into Paris at night, after all that! I could meet you at my father's house, where you came

177

before, near Orléans. He and my stepmother are skiing at the moment. It would be better, at least make the journey a little shorter, and then we can deliver the van into Paris on Sunday, when the traffic is not so bad. Then I could bring you to my apartment. What do you think?'

Megan feels the muscles of her face relax. 'That sounds like a great idea. Thank you, it's very thoughtful of you... Oh, shit the red light is flashing. We're about to be cut off. See you there, then?'

'Yes. See you there. *Au revoir.*'

She can hear the smile in his voice: *'Au revoir,'* she replies to it, softly. And blows a kiss along the abruptly deadened wire.

*

The *autopista* is expensive – particularly because it runs roughly parallel with the older, free *carretera* – but it is smooth, many-laned, and dives through mountains and over valleys. Megan settles the van into a steady clip, sitting comfortably in the slow lane. She listens to tapes left in the back of the glovebox by some other (surely female) hirer of the van – a Janis Ian one, a tinny Tina Turner, and a soaring Karen Carpenter. Listening over and over to the moaning voices of the women, singing of love and loss, and guiding the rumbling van past winter fields of stark plum trees and knotted vines, looming mountain ranges and tracks of barren plain, she feels strangely moved. Perhaps it is the fact that the ageing, wrecked face of Spain gradually transforms as she leaves its tourist strip behind, that she can in her imagination conjure up the lost grandeur of the Iberian Peninsula as it once was: the proud queen of a vast and treasure-hauled empire. Or perhaps it is the voices of the sad, soulful women, disillusioned or disappointed by the failure of romantic love, making the attainment of love itself seem even more poignant and desirable, even if it is, in the end, lost.

*

She stops overnight in Valencia, then starts driving again before day-break. She camps the second night just over the Spanish-French border, at a little town called le Boulou. On Saturday morning, she takes the French autoroute as far as Beziers, before swinging onto the N9, and heading north, towards Orléans.

22

Roses

It is quite dark when Megan approaches Orléans. Her head buzzes with fatigue: the concentration on the winding roads over the Massif Central, coupled with snow drifts and increasing cold, have made her almost mesmerised. When she stops outside Luc's father's house, the van is not the only thing to utter a deep, shuddering sigh.

There are lights behind the thick-paned windows Megan remembers belong to the kitchen. A moon like a swung scimitar glints silver on the dark, fractured glass of the other windows, and makes luminous the ankle-deep snow on the lawn. The air is still and cold: Megan's breath clings gently to the door as she raises her hand to the knocker.

'Hi.' Megan smiles stiffly, hardly able to lift the corners of her mouth, despite her quickened pulse.

Luc says nothing: he looks at her with the yellow light from the foyer behind him falling on her leather-gloved hands and bulky anorak, her stooped shoulders, and her pale wedge of hair and paler face. He says nothing, just holds out his two hands and takes hers and draws her inside. He pushes the door closed behind her, then slips his arms around her cold anorak and draws her mouth to his. And yes, she thinks, as his warm, mint-scented breath and warm, wet mouth move over the cold planes of her face, there are times when words would just get in the way.

*

Later, Megan dreams she is in a rose garden. The air is warm and fragrant around her, and the grass under her feet is soft and hot. She is in a maze of rose gardens; she wanders among them, aimlessly at first, transfixed by their colours, their prickly, pepper-dusted hearts – but then she realises that she can't seem to find a way out of the maze, that all the corridors between the rows of flowers lead only to other corridors. She feels panic; she begins to run: she can see the road that she needs to get to, but she can't find a way through the bushes which have become thorny now – although of course they always were, she just hadn't noticed the thorns – and which tear at her clothes and her skin,

She wakes with a start. She is in a double bed with a heavy feather duvet over her and Luc's body curved around her back. On the bedside table there is a delicate pottery bowl of dried rose petals: it was them she could smell in the dream.

She sighs. The bedroom is warmed by central heating, but even so the air above her face is cool. The curtains are open: moonlight falls in white tiles on the carpet. She is reminded of the castle turret, all those years ago, when she was twenty and she had first desired Luc: of staring at a similar patch of white moonlight, not conscious of it at the time, only aware of the thick, strong desire in her blood, making her limbs weak, making her reason foolish.

She looks over her shoulder at Luc now, a real Luc, whom she can touch and smell and see. She looks at his peaceful face; at the finely-muscled, pale arm with its long hand resting on top of the covers, over her hip; at the smooth, hairless skin on his shoulder and the soft fall of shadow-streaked hair across his forehead onto the pillow. And she thinks, this is real. He is here, with me now, now. But how long before this is all just memory? It's the same feeling of powerlessness she remembers having as a child about a gold ring with a heart shaped into it that her mother had given her, a ring like the one she had watched covetously for nearly six months on the hand of the girl she sat next to at school: a feeling of, I own it, I have it, I can touch it, it is real *now* – but how long before I lose it? How can I stop myself from losing it, and not being able to touch it again? And of course she had lost it.

Lost the mother who gave it to her, too; but that was before she lost the ring. That had been quick, an accident – no premonition there. Perhaps that was why she had been so hopelessly certain about the ring.

She lies on her back, watching Luc's face and frowning. She stops herself thinking about the ring and about her mother; she concentrates on puzzling over her dream instead. What did it mean? That, after all, subconsciously, she wants to escape Luc? She sees him as a trap? If not, where is she trapped? Where is the rose garden? Spain? France? Her job, which seems so successful? Or is she simply trapped in her own desires, which will have inevitable thorns?

Luc stirs, and rolls over, away from her. She curls herself around his back, pressing her naked breasts against his warm skin, and slips her hand onto his lightly furred chest. He seems to be asleep, yet he catches her fingers in his and touches them to his lips.

She lies quietly for a while, feeling his body breathing, until her fingers begin to cramp. Then she removes her hand from his, settles it along her own side, and falls back to sleep.

*

'So, you will stay with me in Paris for some days?'

They are sitting at the kitchen table, a solid timber bench etched with grainy lines and pitted with black spots, but almost cushiony under Megan's elbows. Its edges are curved with age and its colour is a rich honey.

Megan dips a buttery crust of bread into her coffee bowl and curls hair away from her cheek, behind an ear, before answering. 'I'm not sure. You have to go back to work tomorrow, don't you?' She bites the crust, leaning over the bowl so the crumbs fall into it.

'Yes. But we can go out, in the evenings. And tonight there is a party – it's the same, every year, the night before school starts again. I can… *display* you. Is that the word? My Australian friend.' He smiles, his dimple deep. His hair is washed and shiny blond, combed back from his forehead neatly, but already beginning to spring forward.

Megan smiles back and drinks from her bowl. 'If you like.'

'They'll all be teachers, of course.'

'That's okay. I have a rather Eastern attitude towards teachers – that their profession is perhaps the most important of them all, in terms of the handing on of culture and wisdom.'

'Ah,' Luc says, lifting his coffee bowl in salute. 'You see? You have become romantic.' But he looks pleased.

*

Megan follows Luc's red Renault into Paris along the N20, through Angerville and Etampes. They enter the city via Porte d'Orléans, that at least Megan is aware of – but she loses her sense of direction in her concentration on keeping up with him once the traffic thickens. She is quite surprised, therefore, when she recognises the name of the company from whom she hired the van quite suddenly in front of her.

The van is cleaned and tidied, Megan's one suitcase packed into the boot of the Renault, so she is quite quickly out of the warm, leathery-smelling hire-car office. She slips just a hint of regret at the van's mustard sides as Luc edges the nose of the Renault back into the traffic, and she lifts her hand in what might be a faint wave, or only a smoothing of her hair away from her eyes as they drive away.

*

Luc's apartment is in Montparnasse. It is on the second floor of an elongated, whitewashed building crammed into a jumble of similar, but nevertheless markedly individual, such buildings, all jostled together like the leaves of a broken concertina, or a row of mismatched Siamese twins. Parked cars line one side of the street, there are ornate street lamps suspended serenely like watchful swans over the narrow road, and winter-branched trees are spaced evenly from square patches along the concrete footpath. Snow lies on everything. The sky is grey and a chilly wind flips her hair as Megan locks and slams the car door.

'Well,' she says, folding her arms around her as Luc lifts her suitcase from the car boot, 'don't you live in the trendy part of town!'

Luc grimaces. 'Wait until you see how it is inside.'

And yes, she admits: it's not much. A bed, a bench with coffee things, a small refrigerator, a gas ring. Two scuffed leather armchairs, a small, round, pretty-legged table with matching chairs. Crockery and glasses on a tea towel, lining the wall beside the gas ring. A guitar in a corner. Apparent but inefficient central heating, and an electric bar heater, which Luc turns on immediately.

'You know, I believe you now.'

Luc raises his eyebrows in surprise. 'Believe me?'

'Yes. About not having a girlfriend. No sign of her here.'

Luc picks up a pile of clothes which are heaped in a corner of the room, and drops them onto one of the chairs. Then he pauses and looks at Megan silently, frowning.

'Oh, look, I'm just teasing you!' Megan steps toward him and touches him hurriedly on the hand. 'Luc? Really.'

He keeps looking at her, frowning, and she thinks, why? Does he think I don't trust him, or that I think his place is a mess? But he doesn't explain: he simply suddenly grimaces and squeezes her hand. There are many things about him, she thinks then, that I know nothing about. Many things to learn. She watches his eyes soften, the corners of his mouth lift slightly.

He places his greatcoated arms around her. He drops his head to her upturned face and begins to kiss it. 'We can get warm in the bed,' he murmurs into her hair, his face relaxing into hers, his arms moving strongly around her ribs, her hips. 'Then go out to have lunch in a restaurant. Come back to bed again...'

There is no more talk of girlfriends.

*

Luc takes her to the back of a burgundy-walled restaurant which seems to Megan a bit too expensive for him to habituate. But he seems to know the menu: he explains the soup and more complicated main courses. She leans back in the luxury of his decision making, watching the ease with which he orders, tries wine, unfolds his napkin. She notices the irritation she used to feel with him is gone. Perhaps it's because

I'm relaxed, she thinks. I don't have to prove anything any more. Perhaps it's the lovemaking. Or perhaps he's beginning to trust me and is less evasive, and me, him.

Over the third glass of wine and a richly flavoured plate of venison, she begins to tell him about Dickson. She hadn't meant to, but the story comes out suddenly, almost before she realises she has started on it. He listens to her, nodding, chewing, watching her face flutter with anger, animation, glee.

At the end, he picks up his glass and drinks thoughtfully. He says, 'So this story will make you famous?'

'For a little while, I imagine. Should score me brownie points, anyway.'

'Sorry?'

'Make people respect me as a journalist. Give me credibility and bargaining power. Help me get other jobs.'

The waiter appears then, with salad and fresh plates, and by the time he is finished serving, the subject is dropped; but Megan notices Luc seems a little distracted at intervals throughout the rest of the afternoon.

*

The party is in Pigalle, on the right bank of the Seine, near Montmartre. It is as well, Megan thinks, that Odette and I did that clothes wash in Alicante, otherwise I'd be scraping for something clean to wear. At the thought of Odette and the van, she sighs a little.

There's a bath that three of the apartments share, down the hall from Luc's room. Megan washes quickly in it, aware of movement outside, of footsteps on the thinly carpeted floorboards. She applies eye make-up and a little rouge in the glass of a dimly lit, scratched mirror. She has only jeans, clean warm underclothing, a clean shirt and her anorak to wear. But she shrugs. It's probably what she would choose to wear anyway.

*

They have a drink and a plate of fried potatoes and small fried fish in a clattery, coffee-scented, Gitane-pungent café a few streets from Luc's apartment. Megan has no appetite, but Luc is hungry again. When the plates are empty, Luc buys a litre of wine and swings his guitar in its case over a shoulder, and they step out into the glimmering snow, under the pollen halos of the swan-necked street lamps, and follow the drift of their whitened breath to the Montparnasse metro.

23

Frailty

The party is in an apartment, but a much larger one than Luc's. The ceilings are high and plastered ornately, giving the rooms a shabbily elegant air, Megan thinks, sipping her wine and only half listening to Luc talking to a black-moustached art teacher and a tall intense maths one. She feels a bit drunk. Her back aches a little, from standing too long. The room is smoky and dimly lit with red-shaded lamps, and the music, American rock and roll, is loud: they invited the neighbours, Luc told her, so no one complains.

Earlier, Megan was included in conversations: she was asked politely about Australia and her job, how she knew Luc, et cetera – but now they're onto local politics and she having trouble keeping up. The guitar's been abandoned in a corner: perhaps Luc will play it later, at the end, Megan thinks vaguely. But at the moment the party gives no sign of quietening. The room is crowded, and some couples are dancing, bumping into each other but moving their feet neatly.

She is standing beside a velvet-draped window. She parts the curtain with her hand holding the glass, absently. There is snow on the windowsill: in the faded light from the room it has a faint pink glimmer. She looks out for the moon, but can see none, only a black-grey wedge of sky between two apartment roofs. In one of the apartments, she can see the lights of a Christmas tree. Bad luck, she thinks automatically, to leave it up after New Year. But perhaps some children cannot bear to take it down. She remembers that feeling: it always seemed so long until the next Christmas, so long to wait again. Until one year you stopped looking forward to it, at least with the same breathless excitement, and all the magic of it, you find one year, has disappeared...

She lets the curtain fall closed again and looks back at Luc, at his thoughtful frown, one hand on his chin, the other crossed over his waist, dangling an empty glass, his fringe falling gently forward, and she feels a surge of gratitude toward him. He has behaved well, she thinks: looking after her, introducing her as 'a famous Australian journalist' – in French of course – putting an arm around her on occasions. Making it obvious that they are a couple. And their day, this day he had given her – such a lovely day, full to the brim with good things: love-making, food, wine, sleep; and now this, an acknowledgment to his circle of her existence, her present place in his life.

There was only one time he stiffened. A large-eyed, sleek-haired brunette with fine, ironic eyebrows had smiled coldly at him in passing. He hadn't spoken to her, but Megan had been aware of his subsequent glances in her direction, of his long fingers lifting hair back from his face uneasily when she was in the room. But she had not stayed long.

So many things, Megan thinks now, to find out about his past. And he about mine. And perhaps we will.

She sways a little, looking at Luc's face: he is speaking rapidly and she can't follow what he's saying. She's drunk a lot of wine – from nervousness initially, then because there always seemed to be some in her glass. She thinks, I haven't seen his bad side yet. Or he mine. But of course, neither of us probably ever will. Because I'm going home in a couple of days. But I could come back. For a real holiday. If he wants me to.

Of course he wants me to. Free sex, no ties. Fantasy. But could lead somewhere. Good, could lead somewhere good…

Oh, she sighs, that dream again. That dream of a future. That dream, that desire, that longing for something fragile and beautiful and suddenly made, without real effort, without conscious thought, with only inspiration and primitive, childish joy and absorption and delight… Sandcastle dream. Sandcastle dream. Perpetually built in her mind, then washed away again. Always, always washed away in the past…

Because of course, love, life, is not like that.

But still, dreams. What if she stopped dreaming dreams? What then? Nothing. Death.

Dreams. Illusions, sometimes so frail the least playful push could crumble them. But still, necessary. Because they lead to hopeful futures. But even their failure necessary, in fact. Because it helps us to accept the ultimate failure of everything in life, the impermanence of whatever is built into a life – *and to realise the value of the transient for its own sake.*

'All life is, is experience,' she says aloud.

Luc stops mid-sentence and turns to her. 'I'm sorry?' he says, tilting his head so his hair brushes the shoulder of his coat.

She smiles at him, and he sees that her eyes shine, brim with joy, all their habitual cynicism flooded out.

'I was just thinking out loud,' she says. 'It's nothing.' But she keeps looking at him, the smile still in her eyes, tilting her head at him too, so they reflect each other's pose: watching his face, the fall of his hair, the curve of his cheek in the rosy light, the slow answering smile creasing his eyes.

'*Il faut rentrer?*' he asks, softly. Is it necessary to return?

'Yes,' she says. 'Oh, yes.'

About the Author

Tracey-Anne Forbes has had numerous stories and poems published in Australian literary magazines and anthologies, including *Hope* 2022 ACU Prize for Poetry, *Award Winning Australian Writing* 2012 and *One Book Many Brisbanes* 6 (2011). She has had three previous books published by Ginninderra Press: *Crushed Sugar: Stories*; *Saving Ginia: a Verse Novel*; and *Dangerous Places* (a novel). She lives in Brisbane, Australia.

Find out more at http://tracey-anneforbes.webs.com

www.ingramcontent.com/pod-product-compliance
Lightning Source LLC
Chambersburg PA
CBHW051226210726
48290CB00003B/822